Praise for Secret of the Shadows.

" *A spine tingling, unputdownable novel that will keep you guessing till the end.*"

" *a nerve tingling novel with breath taking cliffhangers.*"

" *pulsing with atmosphere and mystery, the writing is so vibrant you can almost hear the tapping of the keys as you turn the pages. Thrilling.*"

And for Out of the Depths.

" *A spooky and exciting story... with also a clever twist at the end which will make the reader rethink the whole story.*"

"Anything by Cathy MacPhail is unputdownable." Julia

Donaldson

2

SCARRED TO DEATH

BY

CATHY MACPHAIL

A TYLER LAWLESS MYSTERY

ALSO IN THE TYLER LAWLESS SERIES

OUT OF THE DEPTHS

SECRET OF THE SHADOWS

THE DISAPPEARED

4

The wind woke me up. Whistling through the window, rattling the panes. We'd been warned on the news of high winds, and mum had told me to make sure my window was closed tight. I'd forgotten. I turned over, pulled the duvet over my head, trying to ignore that wind. Of course I couldn't. Visions in my head of the window being flung wide, crashing against the wall, glass smashing. I gave up in the end, and stumbled out of bed. I was still half asleep as I reached for the handle, to lock it shut. What I saw when I opened my eyes brought me wide awake in a second.

She was there, outside the window, the scarred girl, floating toward me. Her nightgown billowed around her, stained with what looked like blood. She floated like something out of a dream. Like something out of a nightmare. Her face so white, her eyes so dark and deep, the scars on her arms, from wrist to elbow, a livid red. My breath came in short bursts, my mouth was dry as dust. The girl's long fair hair flew in the wind, as if it was alive. Closer she came, till I could see every mark on her face. She was bruised, her cheek swollen and scratched. As if she'd been in some terrible fight. She didn't smile. And that only made her more terrifying. Closer she came, and closer and only the glass was between us. I could see my own terrified reflection merging into her face until it was lost and I became her. She opened her mouth, and there was only blackness inside there. I felt as if I was staring into hell.

' Help me.'

A cry of desperation.

And right at that moment the wind caught at my window and flung it wide. I fell back, sure she was about to leap inside the room toward me, but when I dared look again, the scarred girl was gone.

CHAPTER 1

The scarred girl haunted me more than any of the other ghosts who had appeared to me. Who was she? And how was I supposed to help her?

She looked so sad, and yet, there was something frightening about her too. Sad, as if there was no hope left in her. Frightening, as if she would do anything to escape wherever she was. I could not get the image of her out of my mind.

That first night I had seen her had been at Mac's birthday party, holding out her scarred arms to me, her face so pale, her eyes sunk deep and black. She was so young, only a few years older than me, and she begged, as they all did. 'Help me, Tyler.'

She seemed to be in my head all the time. Her voice whispered to me constantly. 'Help me.'

She came to me on so many nights after that, this girl. Sometimes, she would be a half vision in a dark corner of my room. Sometimes, all I could see was her ghostly face at my window. Once I even turned in my bed to find her standing close beside me. She always wore the same long white night gown, stained with blood. Her own blood surely, from those deep ragged scars.

One night I woke up and she was standing at the bottom of my bed. I drew the duvet up to my chin, and tried to control my fear. Because I *was* afraid, even after seeing so many ghosts, I was still always afraid. I held my breath. She said nothing, only moved around the bed toward me with stumbling steps. She raised her hands and blood dripped from her wrists, as if they were freshly slit. I sat up in bed, more terrified than I had ever been. Her dark eyes made her look like a ghoul, dead, but not dead. I clutched at my duvet, pulled it tighter around me.

' Who are You?' I don't even know how I managed to say the words. I didn't expect an answer, just those same words. 'Help me.'

She opened her blue lipped mouth and I waited for her to speak. And she did, eventually. But she didn't ask me to help her, not this time. Instead she said, and the words came out in one ghostly breath. ' Hayley Brown I am Hayley Brown.' She said it slowly, deliberately, as if she was afraid I might forget. As if it was taking all her strength to say that name. ' Hayley Brown,' the name like a gasp of dead breath, ' Hayley Brown,' she said again. And then, she was gone.

****

Seconds after she'd disappeared I was out of bed. I stared at the carpet, sure it would be soaked with her blood. The carpet was clean, not a mark on it. I whispered into the dark of my room.

' I'll find you, Hayley.' I knew I had no choice. She wouldn't leave me be until I did.

I couldn't go back to sleep, not then. I switched on my bedside lamp, and lifted my laptop and sitting cross legged on the bed I opened it. I googled her name.

Hayley Brown.

Hayley Brown: an award winning pharmacist in Florida

Hayley Brown : a starlet in the 1950's in Hollywood.

Hayley Brown : who had her own business making soft toys.

Too many Hayley Browns.

I sat and thought for a moment. So far, the dead who had contacted me had always lived in my own vicinity. Ben Kincaid, had been a boy in my school. Sister Kelly, the evil nurse, had lived in a little bungalow down the river, and Miss Baxter too, my old teacher from Grovepark, had lived hardly a bus ride away. All of them were practically local. So perhaps this Hayley Brown had lived and died somewhere around here.

Died here.

It was the deaths in the area I should be checking out.

It didn't take me long after that to find the Hayley Brown I was sure I was looking for. A death, fifteen years ago. Hayley Brown. Her death had made a small item in the local paper. She had died at a residential school, Bonaventure House, in a village not far from here, and she had died under suspicious circumstances. At first, I thought 'residential' meant she had gone to some kind of exclusive boarding school. But on another link, in another article in another paper, I discovered that Bonaventure House wasn't any kind of posh boarding school where rich girls were educated. It was a residential school for problem teenagers. The girls who were sent there were too young to be sent to prison. They were locked in. Locked up. And Hayley Brown had been one of them.

Hayley Brown had been convicted of a terrible assault. She had attempted to kill her baby brother. That was all it said. She had spent two turbulent years in Bonaventure House before she had been found dead in a locked room. She had cut her wrists with the knife found lying beside her. She looked as if she had been in a terrible fight too. And I thought of the face I had seen, with its bruises and scratches. Her death had been recorded as suicide, because there seemed no other way to explain it, but there had always been a question mark over it and the truth had never been discovered. How had she managed to get the knife? How did she end up battered and bruised? It remained a mystery that had never been completely solved. Hayley Brown had died alone, guilty of a terrible crime, and now she was back, and she wanted me to help her.

CHAPTER 2

Jazz was my fund of information for everything that went on around this town. She knew everyone and everything, and what she didn't know, her mother did. I sometimes didn't know what I would do without her.

' Bonaventure House?' she said next day when I asked her about it. ' They used to call it the home for bad girls.' Then she giggled.

Adam standing nearby called over. ' Perfect place for you then.'

Quick as a flash Jazz shot right back. ' I'd get sent there if I murdered you.'

Aisha asked. ' I didn't know we had a place like that near here.'

' Not so near, Aisha,' Jazz told her. ' It's in Bracken.' Bracken was a village fifteen miles away. 'Any way, it's not really like that now. It's called an Open Unit. Nobody gets actually locked in. ' She thought about that. ' Well, not that I know of anyway.'

' Why do you want to know?' Mac asked.

I was already prepared for the question. Had a stock answer. ' I was thinking of writing a story about a place like that. You know, for our English project.'

We were doing a project called Trapped, and let's face it, you don't get more trapped than prison.

'I'm doing mine on a zombie attack,' Adam said.

'No surprise there,' answered Jazz.

' I just thought it would make a good story,' I sounded feeble.

' Our Tyler, always writing a story,' Callum said, slipping in beside Aisha. She turned and smiled at him.

I loved how he called me ' our Tyler.' Since my first day at St. Anthony's these friends had welcomed me , included me in everything, and I loved them for it. But actually, Callum was wrong, I was never writing a story. Not anymore. I never had time. Not with all these ghosts crowding in on me. I was too busy trying to figure out how I was supposed to help them.

The bell rang and we began filing inside the school. Jazz whispered. ' I'll find out all I can about Bonaventure House. Okay?' Then she added. ' As long as you tell me the truth about why you want to know.'

I would have to tell Jazz. Jazz knew I had a gift, but she had one too. I was sure of it. Jazz had feelings, intuitions, I don't know how to describe it, but Jazz definitely had a gift. So I knew I could tell her at least a little bit of the truth. But not all. Never all. 'I'll tell you at lunchtime,' I said.

We avoided the cafeteria and the others at lunchtime so we could be alone. Jazz and I sat on the wall outside the school. It was October, and the trees were turning golden brown, and crisp leaves lay on the path. The gargoyles on the old school building seemed to be watching us with menacing interest.

' Ok, tell all,' Jazz said, munching on a packet of crisps. ' I won't say a word. I'm dying to hear what you've got to tell me. I know *I've* got a kind of gift. I feel things... but not like you. Nothing like you, Tyler. You see things, you actually see things. It's so amazing. So come on, tell me why you want

to go to Bonaventure House. Have you seen something happening there?'
Her face was alive with excitement. 'Have you seen one of your ghosts? Go
on, go on, tell me!'

She always made me laugh. ' I will, if I can get a word in edgeways!'

Jazz clamped a hand over her mouth. 'Oops, typical Jazz.' She
mumbled. ' Not a word now. I'll shut up. Go on....Please!!!'

So I told her about Hayley Brown, the scarred girl, and how she had
come to me holding out those scarred arms, asking me to help her. I told
her too all that I had found out about her on the internet.

' So you can see why I have to go to Bonaventure House. '

' But how can you help her? She's dead.'

That was the thing Jazz couldn't know, would never know. She
would never know exactly what my special gift was, because once I had
helped Hayley, once I had put things back the way they were meant to be,
changed her past, changed her death, everything would be different, Jazz
would forget it all. It would never have happened for her. Anyway, she
never needed an answer. Jazz always supplied her own.

She snapped her fingers. ' I know. She hasn't been able to move on. Suicides are always trapped between this world and the next. It's a well known fact.' Then she beamed a smile at me. ' Which I just made up.' She tossed her head.' Anyway, you have to find out the truth. Why she did it? You have to help her.'

' So you'll find out about Bonaventure House for me?'

I didn't even have to wait for the answer to that one. I knew Jazz would. Too excited to stop.

'You can rely on your trusty Dr. Watson!' she said.

CHAPTER 3

Over the next couple of days I waited for Hayley Brown to appear again. She didn't, not the way she had before, night after night, in plain view, and yet, I felt she was with me all the time. It was as if she was always there in the corner of my vision. I'd think I'd see her, moving beside me, and I'd swivel round and she would be gone.

On the bus to school I would be sure I could see her, crowded in among everyone else. As I sat in class, she would be there, almost, a shimmer of darkness in a dim corner. Once, as I was waiting in the queue in the canteen I was certain she was standing just behind me. I turned abruptly and hit Adam with my tray. Chips peas and sausages went everywhere. Adam leapt back.

' What happened there?' he asked me.

' Thought I saw somebody,' I said, and felt my face flush.

Mac was there too. ' Your face is brick red, Tyler.'

That only made me blush all the more, and he whispered. ' I think you suit it.' Then I really did go brick red.

'She wouldn't be Tyler if her face didn't go red,' Adam laughed, and he slipped on the peas and went down on the floor, all arms and legs. Then we were all laughing.

Yet, though I wasn't quite seeing her, I knew she was there, that she would come again. She wouldn't let me go.

My dad picked me up one day after school. He had finished work early for a change.

' You look clean,' I said. Dad's a motor mechanic, he's usually covered in oil, his face smudged with grease.

' No choice Tyler, taking your mum out tonight, remember?'

' Ah, the anniversary. At least this year you didn't forget.'

' Didn't get a chance with your mother leaving clues all over the house.'

I was laughing as I pulled down the mirror above my window, to check my hair. And there sitting in the back seat, was Hayley Brown, her dark rimmed eyes just staring at me.

I let out such a yell, I dropped my can of coke and it splashed all over the seat.

' Tyler!' Dad said. ' Watch my good suit!'He threw me a cloth . ' What happened there?'

I took the cloth silently, didn't even answer him-because when I glanced back Hayley Brown was gone.

Why was she scaring me so much? Was she doing it deliberately? Was she growing impatient waiting for me to help her?

Give me time-I wanted to say-give me time.

It was the morning after the incident in the car that I found Jazz waiting for me at the school gates, a big smile spread across her face.

' When you need a helping hand, just ask Jazz.' She almost sang the words out.She linked her arm in mine and we began to walk up the long drive to school. ' You wanted to know about Bonaventure House, well, I can do even better. We're going there.'

' Going where?' Adam appeared as if from nowhere.

' We're going to Bonaventure House, Adam,' I told him full of excitement.

' The home for bad girls? Can I come?' He wiggled his eyebrows, like some leering Victorian villain.

' Me too?' Mac said. ' I think I might like bad girls.'

Jazz gave him such a push he almost fell over. ' Bonaventure House is for girls only. And, anyway, it's not quite a visit.'

' What do you mean?' Adam asked her.

' We're going there to research our project.'

' You're doing a project too? You, Jazz?' Adam grinned. ' This is amazing!'

' You don't have to sound so surprised!' Jazz pulled me on, leaving the boys laughing behind us. She waited till we were well ahead of them before she spoke again. 'I told my mum about our " English project".' She sketched the inverted commas with her fingers. ' And it turns out my mum used to go there. Can you believe the coincidence! She still keeps in touch with some of the staff there. When I said you wanted to see inside the place, It was her suggested she'd ask her friend if we could go . So she phoned Sister Philomena, that's her friend, and she says we can come on Saturday. Around 12. We can get the bus right there! And you can ask all your questions about....' she hesitated, checking to make sure Adam hadn't caught up with us and was close by, listening, '.... eh, about your project.'

I sighed. It was getting me there. But giving up my Saturday? I hoped Hayley Brown was grateful.

CHAPTER 4

' You're actually going there?' Aisha couldn't believe it when we told her during break. ' My mum heard some of those girls have got to be locked in. All day. And you can't ever have more than three of them in one place at the same time. That's how bad they are.'

' Not all of them,' Jazz said. ' You make it sound as if we're going in to a battle zone.'

' I thought you said it was an open unit, Jazz?' Now I was beginning to get worried.

' It is... mostly. But there's a bit that's more...what's the word...secure?'

' That place sounds worse than Alcatraz.' Adam said. ' Girls are definitely worse than boys.'

' Don't worry, we don't want you to come, it would be too scary for you.' Jazz stuck out her tongue at him. She turned to Aisha. ' But I thought you might.'

Aisha took a step back as if she'd hit her. ' Me? I can think of better ways to spend my Saturday.'

Jazz looked at Callum. ' Yeah, I can imagine. Sitting in Starbucks with Rhett Bulter here.'

' Well, you can include me and Mac here out too.' Adam put his arm round Mac's shoulders. 'Right, pal. We're off to football.'

Mac grinned. He had the whitest teeth I had ever seen. ' One of these days our team has got to win, and we want to be there when it happens. Right , mate?' He turned his big brown eyes on me. 'Why on earth do you want to go there, Tyler?'

Jazz put her arm in mine and answered for me. ' If you want to make your work authentic, you have to research it thoroughly. That right, Tyler?'

' Do your research on the internet, like everyone else.' Aisha suggested.

' We'll only have to go once,' I said meekly. ' I hope.'

Mac and Adam fell about laughing. ' Unless they keep you in.'

' I'll come and rescue you, Tyler,' Mac said, and he winked.

' Will you rescue me, Adam?' Jazz batted her eyelashes. Didn't work on Adam. He only laughed.

' I'll send you a cake with a file inside,' he said.

In spite of all the jokes and laughing, I was beginning to get a bit scared even thinking of going there. Jazz brushed my fears aside. Jazz, always the bold one.

' We won't be anywhere near those girls, Tyler. There's only a couple of them in the secure wing. I told you, it's an open unit.' She tutted. ' Honestly, you'd think we were risking life and limb here.' She winked at me.

' Just watch yourself, Jazz.' Adam leaned closer. ' They might mistake you for one of them bad girls, and keep you in.'

And all I could think of was... what was I letting myself and Jazz, in for?

Mum didn't want me to go either. She'd heard stories about the girls there too.

' I'll be with Jazz.' She trusted Jazz, I knew that. She liked her.

' Even Jazz couldn't protect you from that lot.,' she said.

' We're not going anywhere near those girls. And we'll be supervised all the time. Jazz's mum's friend, she's a nun, she'll look after us.'

' Why do you want to use that place for your project anyway?'

I shrugged. I'd been reading more about Bonaventure House on the internet, so I'd learned a little more about it. ' It's got a really interesting history, mum. Wasn't always used as secure accommodation . When it was first opened as a unit way back in the last century, a lot of girls were sent there because they were having babies and weren't married. They had the babies there and then they had to give them up for adoption. Can you imagine how awful that must have been?'

' I still don't understand why you can't find out all you need on the internet. What more are you going to find out by going there ?' she had asked that more than once. But I had to go there. I had to be in the place where Hayley had died, and that, of course, was the thing I couldn't tell her. I couldn't find out about Hayley Brown just on a computer. I needed to see Bonaventure House, and feel the atmosphere of the place where she had died all around me.

' I promise, mum. There won't be any trouble.'

How wrong can a person be?

CHAPTER 5

Jazz and I took the bus to Bracken on the next Saturday morning. The village itself was situated high in the hills above the river, and the higher the bus climbed, the more beautiful was the scenery. It was as if the whole length of the river had been spread out just for us. Bonaventure House was a couple of miles past the village. It was surrounded by high stone walls and seemed to appear like magic just as we came over the final hill, an old Victorian granite building with turrets and crow step gables, standing carved against an azure blue sky. I thought of all the girls who had come here, both in the past and now, who would have been filled with trepidation at the first sight of it.

We were seeing it in sunlight, but all at once a strange thing happened. The scene rippled, the sun disappeared. It was night, and I felt I had become Hayley Brown, seeing it for the first time. I was arriving in darkness, and the first thing I saw was those turrets etched against a moonlit sky. I was struggling with the women who sat in the car with me, one on each side, hemming me in. ' I don't want to go there! I don't want to go there!' I was screaming, and kicking, trying desperately to get out of the car. But it was no use. They were stronger than me. And those turrets were coming ever closer. And once in there, I would be trapped, and the thought terrified me.

' Are you okay?' Jazz shook me back to the present. I felt the sun on my face. I was me again.

' Just thinking of how I would feel if I was going there knowing I couldn't leave.'

But what really scared me was that for those seconds I had become Hayley Brown. I was sure of it.

The bus left us on the main road and we had to walk almost a mile to the main gate. The river was like glass that day and there was a loaded tanker sailing down, cutting the water. A rainbow curved from one side of the river to the other, like a frown. Like a warning to stay away from here. Why was I thinking a thing like that about something so beautiful as a rainbow? I didn't want to be here. if I could I would turn round now and just go home.

There was a train travelling up the shore line heading for the city. It looked just like a toy train. Hard to imagine people were sitting on that train, living breathing people with plans for the day. Some of them perhaps, looking across and seeing us as only tiny ants. I so wished I was on that train.

Jazz nudged me. ' Always in a dream, Tyler.'

She was right. I was. I found it easy to lose myself in my thoughts. ' Sorry,' I said.

Bonaventure House could have passed for some grand old country estate, except for the candy striped barrier at the gate, and the security guard. He asked who we had come to see and Jazz, quite boldly, told him we were here on 'official business'. She said it without a blush, as if she was some important visitor. That made the man smile. 'Sister Philomena knows we're coming,' she told him. He went back into his booth and lifted the phone and called someone, I took it that it was Sister Philomena herself, because he put down the phone and said. ' Just go right in.' He pointed up the driveway. ' To the main house there. Sister Phil will be waiting for you.' Then he let us pass behind the barrier and into the grounds of Bonaventure House.

We walked up a long path to the main house. The path was bordered by trees, and though the morning was beautiful, it had been raining all night and the branches still dripped with rain. The sky was blue now, but there were ominous black clouds heading our way. Was that another message for me? Bad things were coming?

' Great day to go ghost hunting,' Jazz said.

She was right. I knew I was waiting for something to happen. Waiting for Hayley Brown to suddenly step out in front of us.

As we cleared the trees we could see well tended gardens and lawns, and the path split to lead to a small house on the left, and further down past the gardens a modern glass extension had been added on to another older building. But we were heading for the main house, with high Victorian windows on the ground floor and narrow slats of windows on the floor above, and even tinier attic windows built into the roof.

' It looks creepy outside, doesn't it? As if it could house a thousand ghosts,' Jazz said. 'But Mum says it's bright and cheerful inside.'

It was then I remembered Jazz telling me that her mum used to come here. ' Why did your mum come here?' I asked.

Jazz giggled. ' She wasn't one of the inmates! What do you think my mum is!' she pulled me on. 'No, believe it or not, when she was a little girl my mum wanted to be a nun.' That sent her giggling again. ' Imagine, my mum a nun! ' Jazz's mum was dark and pretty and never without a boyfriend. Jazz's dad had died a long time ago.

' So what changed her mind?' I asked.

Jazz was quick with her answer. ' She discovered boys! Anyway, she used to come here with her youth club to help the nuns. Sister Phil was one of the nuns who was here at the time.'

Jazz's mum always surprised me. Wild on one side, and so kind and thoughtful on the other. Just like Jazz.

' So, Sister Phil will remember Hayley Brown?'

Jazz grinned. ' Exactly.'

There was more security when we came to the main house, a CCTV camera above the door seemed to be watching our every move. Jazz rang the buzzer. A moment later the door was opened by a smiling woman and it took me a moment to realise she was actually a nun. She wasn't wearing a habit, but a grey dress, and a white scarf tied round her head. She wasn't young, yet her skin was smooth and clear, her eyes were bright. ' Jasmine! You look so much like your mum!' The nun's eyes turned to me. ' I'm Sister Philomena. But everyone calls me Sister Phil.'

So this was Jazz's mum's friend. I held out my hand. ' I'm Tyler. Tyler Lawless.'

' Well, come this way, both of you.'

I whispered to Jazz as we followed her. ' I didn't know it was still run by nuns?'

' It isn't,' she whispered back. ' Mostly social workers now, but Sister Philomena is still involved.'

' Do you think she'll tell us anything about Hayley Brown?'

Then her voice became even softer. ' If we ask her nicely.'

' That would have been fifteen years ago...she looks too young to have been here that long.'

Jazz's answer was a giggled whisper. ' Good living, that's what keeps her looking like that.'

Sister Philomena led us along a long corridor asking after Jazz's mum and her sisters as she walked. The corridor was a mixture of dark panelled wood, and brightly painted walls. So old, and yet, I had never seen anywhere so clean. Not a speck of dust on a window sill, not a mark on the windows. The only dust you could see were the dust motes that danced in the beams of pale sunlight. The corridors were painted so white they made you blink, and there were fresh flowers on every sill. We could see where they had come from, in the gardens outside where some late flowers were still in bloom.

' We have lovely gardens, and of course we have a gardener on staff, ' Sister Philomena said, when she saw us stop to admire them. ' Some of the girls enjoy taking care of them too, and some are so good at arranging flowers. I always say. Everyone has a talent, if they can just find it.'

But walking along the corridor we saw not another soul. And the place seemed so silent. 'Where are the other girls?' I asked.

'They're in a separate section of the house,' she said. 'They all have their chores to do, even on a Saturday. It will be visiting time soon. Most of them have family coming.'

We followed Sister Phil into a big kitchen. Another woman was there, her sleeves rolled up to the elbow, her hands deep in suds. She looked older than the nun, and her body was chubby with fat. She turned and smiled at us as we came in. 'So, this is your friend's girls?'

Sister Phil said. 'Yes, Annie, this is Jasmine, and this is Tyler. They're writing a school project called Trapped. Isn't that right, Jasmine?'

Before Jazz could answer, Annie said. 'Oh, it'll be a horror story if you're writing about this place.'

Sister Phil tutted. 'Oh, don't listen to Annie.'

'Why should they? Nobody else does.' Annie said.

Sister Phil smiled at us. 'We thought you might like to stay for some lunch. We're just getting lunch prepared if you'd like to help us?'

I nodded eagerly. 'Oh, I don't mind at all.'

'Could you peel potatoes? Cut vegetables?'

' We could lay the tables too.'

' No, no, the girls can do that themselves'

' But they can't peel potatoes?' Jazz asked .

Annie snorted. ' You don't dare let some of them near anything sharp.'

Sister Phil almost shouted at her. ' Annie! You'll scare the life out Jasmine and Tyler. That's not the reason. They often do help in the kitchen.'

Annie only raised an eyebrow. ' Fore warned is forearmed, eh? And with that lot,' she nodded her head in the direction of that new glass extension were the girls were housed, ' armed is something you don't want them to be.'

I tugged at Jazz's sleeve. ' Maybe we should just leave.'

She pulled her arm away. ' This is good research, isn't it? ' She glanced at Sister Phil, afraid she might be listening. ' Anyway, it was you who wanted to come.'

Not me, I wanted to say. I didn't want to come. It's Hayley Brown. I didn't even know how to bring her name into the conversation. Luckily, I had Jazz. She had no such problem.

' I don't think the girls here nowadays are as bad as they used to be, are they Sister?'

' No such thing as bad girls, Jasmine,' she said at once. 'Anyway, it's a different kind of place now.'

'Have you been here a long time?' I asked her.

' Too long probably.' She said. ' But I do have lots of good memories. When I first came, we used to have babies here. It was lovely to have babies here,' she said with a sigh. Then she shrugged. ' Maybe not for the girls though.'

They'd had to give their babies up, I remembered. How sad.

' Unmarried mothers, we called them then. I'm glad we don't call them that now.'

' You had some really bad girls, though, didn't you?' Jazz asked her, pushing her way towards the question she really wanted to ask.

Sister Phil was reluctant to say anything bad about any of them. ' Not bad, Jasmine, troubled. Then and now. Girls who have had terrible lives, and no chances, we try to help them.'

Annie snorted again, but said nothing.

' I heard about one girl, she had a really bad reputation....' I felt myself go red as Jazz pretended to try to remember the name. Screwing up her eyes, tapping her teeth with her nail. ' Hayley Brown?'

Only a slight hesitation as Sister Phil lifted out a stack of plates from the cupboard. But I noticed it. ' How on earth do you know her, Jasmine?'

' Heard the name, did you know her?'

' Hayley was a very troubled girl,' the nun answered. ' I only wish we had been able to help her. And I don't think we would want you to mention her in your project.'

No, they wouldn't, I thought, not someone with such a dark history behind her. One who had died under such mysterious circumstances.

She lifted the plates and carried them out of the kitchen. As soon as she was gone, Annie let out a guffaw. ' Troubled? Too nice a word for that Hayley Brown. Trouble, was what I called her. I remember her okay.'

' You do?' I asked.

Annie turned to us. ' You don't forget a girl like Hayley Brown. She was born bad that one.'

CHAPTER 6

Jazz's eyes went wide. ' Born bad? Just how bad was she?'

Annie began to dry her hands on a tea towel. She glanced to the door to make sure Sister Phil wasn't on her way back. ' Blinking violent, she was. Even before she came here. She attacked her wee brother. Pushed him down a flight of stairs, almost killed him. She tried to stab one of her teachers too. That's why she ended up here. Uncontrollable. A year older she would have been sent to the jail. That's how she was always locked up in here. I'm telling you, we were the last resort. Usually this place can handle anybody. And I've seen some bad ones. But nobody as bad as she was. Nobody could handle Hayley Brown.'

Sister Phil came back in just then, and Annie gave us a wink and turned back to the sink. But the sudden silence must have made Sister Phil suspicious. She must have known we had been talking about Hayley. It was clear Annie enjoyed a gossip. But the nun said nothing. ' Well, girls, what would you like to know for this project of yours? ' She sat at the table and motioned us to join her. ' I'll tell you as much as I can, and when we're done, you can have a little walk round the grounds before lunch.'

We took out our notebooks, and Sister Phil answered our questions about Bonaventure House. We had our set questions all ready.

The house had been left by a rich family to the nuns at a nearby convent to help young girls ' in trouble'.

' Did they all have to give up their babies?' I asked her.

She sighed. ' Most of them. If they'd been sent here by their families, they would have been disowned if they had wanted to keep them. They had no choice.'

' That's so unfair,' Jazz said.

' It was. But it was a different time, different attitudes. And a lot of the babies went to lovely families.'

' When did it start to become a prison?'

Sister Phil gave her such a look. ' It's never been a prison, Jasmine. It's called secure accommodation, and in the 1960's when attitudes began to change about unmarried mothers, we began to take girls in another kind of trouble, but too young to be sent to prison.'

Sister Phil told us everything we needed to know about Bonaventure House itself, but nothing about any of the girls who had stayed there. Nothing about Hayley Brown. It was clear she was someone no one wanted to talk about. Yet, she was the one I had come here for, and I could not leave till I found out something about her.

' I can't give you any specific information about the girls. But I hope being here, will make you think about the girls who come to this place, and can't leave, as you can. The girls who are trapped here. You can write about how we try to prepare them for their freedom, and help them to rebuild their lives.' Sister Phil pointed to our notebooks. ' Why don't you write that down? It's a good quote.'

Here, I was, pretending I was writing a project called Trapped, but in fact, I was the one who was trapped because I wasn't going to get out of here until I knew the facts about Hayley.

' Well, if I've told you enough, ' Sister Phil got to her feet. ' Lunch won't be long.' She glanced out of the window. ' It's still dry, so why don't you have a little wander round the grounds before lunch. Take in the architecture of the building, and our brand new extension. And, of course, our lovely gardens,' she finished proudly.

As soon as she had left the kitchen Annie turned to us, making a show of drying her hands quickly. ' Come on, I'll give you a wee guided tour,' she said. 'Sister Phil, she's lovely, but she hasn't told you any of the good stuff.'

As Annie led us out of the kitchen into the grounds, she waved across to the gardens. ' I keep telling them, they could sell the flowers they grow here. Make a bit of money. They've built these state of the art additions,' she pointed beyond the gardens to the new glass extension, gleaming in the low winter sun. ' Can't take you there I'm afraid. It's out of bounds, just open to the public at visiting times, and you should see the rooms they've got in there, televisions, computers, x boxes. You name it. I'd love a room like the ones they've got, *and!* they've got a beautiful gym, and everything. And this is supposed to be punishment. '

Jazz nudged me, and giggled as we walked behind Annie.

I tried to listen, but all the time my eyes were darting around, I was expecting Hayley Brown to appear round every corner. But there was no sign of her. And more importantly, no sense of her. Apart from that eerie moment when I had felt I had become her, I had no feeling of her presence. I began to wonder why I was here at all.

' What would they call this place now, Annie?'

' Blinkin' holiday camp, if you ask me. ' she snorted. 'A care facility, that's what they like to call it. A molly coddle facility if you want my opinion. What would Sister Phil say? We care for girls whose lives have spiralled out of control. '

Jazz nudged me. ' But some of these girls have caused other people's lives to spiral out of control. Don't forget their victims, eh?'

' You're a girl after my own heart!' Annie said. ' Don't forget their victims. They did a lot of bad things.'

' Like Hayley Brown,' I said softly.

Annie stopped and turned. ' What is this interest you have with Hayley Brown?'

Jazz came to my rescue. ' Tyler went on the internet when she knew we were coming here, to find out about the place.' She touched my arm. ' And Hayley Brown stories are everywhere.'

Annie pursed her lips. 'Well, you heard what Sister Phil said, they won't want you writing a story about Hayley Brown, Tyler.'

I assured her immediately.' No. No, I wouldn't do that.'

She smiled again. ' Oh, I know that. Mind you, if you did have to write a story, I think you should write one with a happy ending.'

' And Hayley Brown's didn't have a happy ending?'

' Well, if you've been on the Internet, you know that already.'

The path we were on separated and veered to the left towards that little isolated house we had had seen coming in. Annie let out a gasp of surprise. ' Wait a minute, that's funny.'

The door of this house was lying open. ' They don't use this place now,' Annie went on. ' It's always kept locked.'

' Why?' Jazz asked.

Annie began heading up the path towards the front door, and we followed her. 'It's where they kept the.... I mean......' She didn't finish. ' It's a lovely little house though,' she went on. ' I think they should do something with it. But then, whoever listens to me?'

' Why do they keep it locked?' Jazz asked, and again, Annie looked reluctant to say anything.

'This was where they put the really bad ones, if you must know. This is where your Hayley Brown died.'

Our Hayley Brown, already it was as if we owned the history of her. And now I knew why that door was lying open. Hayley Brown had made sure of it.

' Do you want to see inside?' Annie glanced around as if she was checking if anyone could see us.

' Can we?' I asked.

' Well, the door's lying open. I'm obliged to go in and investigate.' She hesitated for only a moment. ' Anyway, I don't see the harm in letting you see inside. It's not as if it's a crime scene or anything.'

As we neared the house I couldn't get rid of the feeling I had been here before. I had walked up this path.... no, I had been dragged up this path. I didn't want to go inside again.

(why was I thinking...again? I had never been here before...had I?)

I was afraid. Because I knew what I was going to see. I knew exactly what this house looked like inside.

There would be a long corridor, and a community room at the end with high windows. I could see the sun shining onto the polished wooden floors. And to the left of that room, there was another corridor leading to four rooms. Four rooms with numbers on the doors. I saw it all as clear in my mind as a photograph. We reached the front door, and I stood on the threshold and the long corridor stretched ahead. Exactly as I had imagined it.

You've seen it before, Tyler.

The high windows were of stained glass depicting avenging angels spearing a horned devil. Only the sun wasn't shining this time.

This time...had the sun been shining when I was here before?

Today, the place was dark, the shutters were closed. Annie stepped inside, Jazz followed her.

' Aren't you coming?' Jazz asked when she saw me holding back.

' Of course, I am.' Did my voice tremble? I was sure it did- and I forced myself to step over the threshold, and a feeling such as I had never had before swept over me. A cold icy feeling I could not put into words. Not for the first time that morning, I wanted to turn away. I wanted to run. Was this a warning? A premonition? Or a memory? I couldn't tell, all I knew was that some instinct seemed to be telling me I was making the biggest mistake of my life.

CHAPTER 7

Jazz slipped her arm in mine. ' You went white as a sheet there.' Then before I could say a word she carried on-' not that my mother's sheets are ever white. Red, black, brown, you name it. I don't think there's a white sheet in our house.'

She laughed, so did Annie, and I smiled. She had given me time to collect myself. 'I'm fine, it's just a bit cold in here.' I rubbed at my arms.

' Bound to be cold,' Annie said. ' There's no heating in this place.'

' Why did they put some girls here, Annie?'

' Oh you might as well know. They tried to keep them separate from the others. They were a bad influence on the rest of them. Can you believe that! As if any of them needed a bad influence!'

' Where do you keep those girls now?'

That made Annie laugh again. ' Oh it's all politically correct now. It's an open unit. We can't separate the bad yins. We've got to give them all the kid glove treatment. We've got to be kind.'

' And weren't you kind before?' I asked.

' The sisters always tried to be, I can tell you that. Me? I would have gave them a clip round the ear if I had got the chance.'

We walked down the hall to the community room, devoid of furniture now. There was a big stone fireplace, and old fashioned radiators below the high windows. ' Did they all have their own bedrooms?'Jazz asked.

It was me who answered. ' Yes, there's only four of them. They're down here.'

Jazz and Annie stared at me. ' How did you know that?' Annie asked.

Jazz saved me again. ' Flip, you could find out anything on the internet. Right Tyler.'

Did Annie see me swallow, and pause before I nodded.

' I won't have to tell you then about the special room. Room 4.' Anne said, as she led us down the corridor. Past three of the four bedrooms, each with a lock on the brown painted door. I drew in my breath when I saw the fourth door, the only one with a spyhole. Everything else around me seemed to disappear. The rest of the house fell away. There was no Jazz and no Annie. There was a blackness all around that door. I stopped walking. Yet, even then, it was as if the door was moving toward *me* , coming closer.

The door of Room 4 was bright red. Red like blood, I watched it and waited for it to open and a river of blood to burst through. I heard Jazz's voice come from somewhere far away.

' Why was Room 4 so special?'

I didn't need Annie to answer that. ' This is the one they kept for suicide watches.' It was my voice, somewhere far away.

I heard Annie say. ' Now how did you know that? Internet I suppose. Didn't do Hayley Brown any good though. Because this is where she died, and she did commit suicide.'

And in that moment the door was no longer red. It was brown like the others, and I was standing in front of it with Jazz and Annie on either side of me, and for the life of me I could not remember how I got there.

Jazz let out an excited gasp. ' Can we see inside?'

' ' Fraid not. This is definitely locked,' Annie said. She put her hand on the door knob as if to prove it. ' And I don't have ......' Then it was Annie who gasped.

Because the door to Room 4 swung open.

I didn't want to see inside. I would have run then if I could. I was icy cold, and yet hot at the same time. Some voice inside my head was telling me to run. Get away. I was so afraid.

No fear in Jazz. She was the first to step inside. ' It's just an empty room' she said, her voice tinged with disappointment.

' What did you expect?' Annie said. ' A five star hotel suite? '

Jazz turned back to me. ' Don't you want to see, Tyler?'

I hovered behind because I didn't want to look, yet I knew I had no choice. Hayley Brown had laid this all out for me. She wanted me to be inside this room. I moved to the doorway, still reluctant to take that final step. It was only a bare room now, with no furniture in it. No furniture and only a bleak slash of light coming through the shuttered window. It took all my courage to take that step into the room and in that same instant the room shimmered, and I knew what was happening. I was moving into her time. Hayley Brown's time. Jazz and Annie were no longer there. I blinked and then I could see it as it once had been. There were bright curtains at the window, a single bed with a duvet to match the curtains, a reading lamp on a table beside it, a desk in the corner, and a chair.

And then *she* stepped into view right in front of me. Hayley Brown. Almost as if she'd been hiding, waiting for the best moment to make her entrance. She was so close I almost stumbled back. I had to force myself to stop from screaming. She had the same black eyes, same lank hair, I'd never seen her this close before. My mouth went dry. My teeth began to chatter. ' Help me!' It was a snarl of an order.

'What's wrong, Tyler?' It was Jazz. Suddenly I could see her, standing beside me. Standing beside Hayley. What was happening? It seemed I was in two times at once. In the past, and in the now.

I waited for Jazz to yell out, to scream. Hayley Brown was standing right beside her. It was surely impossible that she couldn't see her. Yet, I knew she didn't. But she felt her. She rubbed at her arms. ' There's a draught coming from somewhere.'

I closed my eyes, and when I looked again, the room was stark and empty, and Hayley Brown was gone.

' What exactly did happen to Hayley Brown, Annie?' Jazz asked.

Annie shrugged. ' Och, you're going to make me tell you, I suppose.' She was relishing being forced. ' She was never out of trouble that one. Attacking people, threatening them, or cutting herself. She was forever harming herself. Looking for attention if you ask me. She even tried to escape once. She was getting worse at the end, began raving. And then, one morning...' Annie shook her head as if she was still couldn't believe the story she was telling us. ' They found her dead, swimming in blood, she'd slit her wrists, and she was all bruised and battered as if she had been in some kind of a fight.'

' Could anyone have gotten into the room during the night.'

' No. There were people on duty, but they heard nothing. They locked her in at night, without a knife anywhere in sight, and in the morning they opened the door....and..' she shrugged again.' There she was, dead, and a knife lying beside her. There was a police enquiry, but nothing came out. '

' So how did she get the knife?' Jazz asked.

Annie nodded. ' Nobody knows. But the way she died, put suspicions on a lot of decent people, as if they'd done something wrong. She didn't leave a note, and the mystery of that knife has always put a question mark over how this place was run, and the people who ran it. Even after she died she made sure people suffered. That's what I mean about being, bad to the bone.'

And I thought of the girl who came to me, with her sad, desperate eyes, and her scarred arms....bad to the bone? There was a mystery here, and Hayley Brown needed me to find out the truth.

Annie went on. She was enjoying telling her story. ' Mind you, Hayley Brown's become something of a legend here,' Her voice became a whisper. ' The girls say she wanders the corridors at night-time, they say they've heard her, they've seen her.'

Jazz nudged me frantically. ' A ghost! She haunts this place?'

' Oh it's all nonsense, but you know how girls are,' Annie said. ' Especially the one's here. She's buried here you know, ' Annie indicated somewhere outside with a nod of her head. ' Out in the old graveyard.'

' Oh, my goodness ,she's still here,' Jazz nudged me again.

Right at that moment we heard the hurried clip of shoes tapping on the wooden floor. Sister Phil swept in, looking not very pleased. 'Annie! What are you thinking about? You're not supposed to let people in here.'

Annie just shrugged. ' The blinkin' door, pardon my French, was lying open. I had to come in to see if there was anybody inside. This door was open as well.' As she spoke she was ushering us out of the room 4.

' Room 4 was open too?' Sister Phil said, puzzled. ' How on earth could that have happened?'

' Well, I'm sure I don't know.' Annie winked at us and strode out ahead of us, not a bit bothered to be caught with us here. I don't think anybody told Annie what to do. And she said again.' I'm sure I don't know.'

' She really shouldn't have taken you in here.' Sister Phil said as we followed Annie out.

'It was our fault...we asked to come in with her,' I said, not wanting Annie to get into too much trouble.

' You wanted to know about Hayley Brown, didn't you?' Sister Phil didn't wait for our answer. 'Well, Annie's is a bit of a storyteller, so I wouldn't' believe too much of what she tells you. ' She smiled again. 'Come on girls. Lunch will be ready in ten minutes. Still okay for staying? ' We both nodded. 'Okay. Have a little wander round the gardens. You'll hear the bell.'

It was Sister Phil who locked the door of the house this time, very carefully, trying the handle two or three times to make sure it was shut tight. Then she went off after Annie. We could hear Sister Phil reprimanding her all the way, and Annie walking on ahead not listening to a thing she said.

' I like that Annie,' Jazz said.

' You would. She's your kind of woman.'

' You saw Hayley Brown in that room, didn't you?' Jazz asked the question she'd been dying to ask.

' She was there, Jazz, just staring at me.'

' Oh, I don't know how you cope with that!' Then she giggled. ' She needs you to find out the truth about how she died. You know that?'

' I know that, Jazz,' I said.

' Just be careful. Maybe Annie's right. If she was that bad in life, she's certainly not an angel now.'

But how could I be careful? And ghosts can't hurt me. I'd proved stronger than the most evil of them, Sister Kelly. I could handle Hayley Brown. At least, that's what I thought.

Jazz pointed beyond the gardens. ' Look, there's the old graveyard. Let's look for Hayley Brown's grave.'

CHAPTER 8

The graveyard was on the hill, and overlooked the river. The monuments and stone angels seemed to be reaching up to the sky in prayer.

' Great view from here,' Jazz laughed. ' Too bad they're all too dead to appreciate it.'

The gravestones were mostly moss covered and old. The writing carved into them too worn to even read. ' I don't think anyone gets buried here now.'

' Health and safety,' Jazz giggled. ' Might be hazardous to your health to be buried here any more.'

Yet the ground around the headstones,   even the very old ones, was kept neat and tidy, the grass trimmed. Out of respect for the people who were buried there, I imagined.

That seemed mostly to be nuns .

Sister Mary Francis

Sister Mary Sebastian

Mother Mary Angelus

Nuns from a century ago and more. But further on we found other graves and these weren't the graves of nuns.

' Hey, look at this one, Tyler.' Jazz called me across to a small stone guarded by an angel.

ELLEN GRANT

AND HER BABY DAUGHTER, LIZZIE

REST IN PEACE.

' There's a story there, Tyler,' said Jazz.

' And a sad one too. I wonder if she died having her baby?' I slid my arm in Jazz's as if we could comfort each other . ' That is so sad.'

' She called her baby, Lizzie,' Jazz said softly.

Perhaps Lizzie had been the mother who deserted Ellen Grant when she found out she was pregnant, yet the mother she still loved, or, perhaps Lizzie was a friend she had made here. Already I was making up a story about Ellen Grant and her baby. They were becoming real to me. I looked at Jazz. Her eyes bubbled with tears.

The bold Jazz had such a soft heart.

' We don't have to look at any more. Do you want to go?' I asked her.

She shook her head. ' No. Come on. You need to help Hayley Brown. Let's see if we can find her grave.'

As I looked across the graveyard, a girl stood up from behind one of the stones. Obviously she had been bending at one of the graves, hidden behind a gravestone. A thin girl, perhaps a couple of years older than we were. She got to her feet and looked right across at us.

I pulled Jazz closer. ' I need you to tell me something. I see a girl standing over there. I need you to tell me that you see her too.'

Jazz didn't look at first. She blinked and stared at me. ' You know how I'm a bit psychic as well,' she said. ' If I see her, it might mean that I can see ghosts too.' She drew in her breath. 'Right. Where is she?'

When I looked, the girl was gone.

' Someone was there...' I began. At that moment, to my relief, she stood up again. Jazz sighed in disappointment. ' I think she's real, you know. I see her too.'

As if she was aware we were both watching her, the girl looked over. She smiled and waved and began to come toward us. Jazz gripped my arm. ' She could be a serial killer for all we know. Has she got a chainsaw under her coat?'

Jazz always made me laugh. The girl had short fair hair, and as she came close we could see had such a pretty baby face. ' Have you just arrived? I've not seen you before? What are you in for?' Questions fired at us so quickly we didn't have time to answer.

' Hey, hold on,' Jazz said. ', we're not in for anything. We're not inmates.'

The girl smiled. ' Neither am I. I'm just visiting.' The girl held out her hand. I saw it was dirty, that there was earth under her fingernails. She saw me glance and drew her hand back. ' Sorry, I was trying to tidy up some of the graves. Put in some seeds, so there'll be flowers next year.'

I almost grabbed at her hand to shake it I felt so embarrassed. ' That's so nice,' I said. ' My name's Tyler.'

' And I'm Jazz,'

' Jazz and Tyler. That's nice. I'm Charlotte....but everybody calls me Charlie.'

' Charlie, I like that.' I looked around the graveyard. ' Do you come here regularly?' I wanted to ask who she was visiting, but it seemed a bit too much of an intrusion.

' To the graveyard?' Charlie nodded. ' Yes, I like them to know they've not been forgotten.'

' You must know everyone here then,' Jazz said.

' Are you looking for someone in particular?'

' Hayley Brown,' I said.

'The ghost! Oh my goodness, you've heard about her?'

Jazz almost jumped with excitement. 'Does she really haunt this place?

'So they say,' Charlie shrugged. 'They say she's been seen walking the corridors, or standing at windows. The girls are terrified of her. She's a malevolent ghost. Evil. They say.'

A chill ran through me. Could that be true? And if it was...what was I doing trying to help a malevolent ghost? Was that why she was making me so afraid?

Charlie looked around as if she thought someone might be listening. 'You can't really talk about her here. Everyone clams up when you ask about her.'

'You don't have to tell us that,' Jazz said. 'We've noticed it, haven't we Tyler?'

'There's a mystery about how she died.' Charlie went on. She obviously wasn't reluctant to discuss Hayley Brown. 'Did you know that?'

'We heard. But I love mysteries,' Jazz said. 'We both do. Tyler here, wants to be a writer.'

Charlie beamed. ' So do I! I've always wanted to be a writer. Well, we could both get a great story out of Hayley Brown.' She began walking, beckoning us to follow her. ' Come on, I'll show you her grave.'

We walked past the graves with the angels and the statues, and the stone memorials, past the graves laid with fresh flowers, sometimes even plastic ones. The ground was uneven and Charlie stumbled against me, and would have fallen if I hadn't caught her. ' Sorry,' Charlie said.

Charlie led us on, heading for one solitary grave, lying by itself. And I felt another chill, but this time it was sadness. Hayley Brown, alone in life, alone in death.

' It looks so lonely,' I said.

' That's what I think too,' Charlie agreed. ' It makes me feel sad, but they say she was buried here to keep her badness from seeping into the other graves.'

Her stone was small and plain.

HAYLEY BROWN

REQUIESTAT IN PACE

And the date of her death, November 27th. Only three weeks from now would be her anniversary.

' **Requiestat in pace.** That's Latin for rest in peace,' Charlie told us. ' But I don't think she does. Not if she really is wandering the corridors, staring out of windows, frightening people. '

' Have you seen her?'

Charlie's face went red. ' Me? No?' Did she say it too quickly, I thought she did.' I only visit here on a Saturday.'

'She committed suicide, didn't she?' I asked.

Charlie looked around her again. Her voice was a whisper. ' Well, that's what they want you to think.'

Cold wrapped itself around me again, as if I had stepped into a refrigerator.

' She was locked in, alone, and in the morning they went inside and found her dead. Her wrists were slit, blood everywhere.' Neither Jazz nor I interrupted Charlie, perhaps she had something else to tell us. Something we hadn't already heard.

' The verdict was suicide, but....they found a knife in the room with her, a knife she hadn't had the night before. A knife belonging to one of the doctors here.   A doctor who hated her. Lots of people think that doctor murdered her. Doctor Crow.'

CHAPTER 9

' Doctor Crow,' I said. ' We haven't heard that name before.'

Charlie went on. ' The knife belonged to her, she was the psychiatrist here. She couldn't say how Hayley got the knife. And, although the verdict was suicide, it ruined her career. Doctor Crow hated Hayley and everyone knew it. Mind you, from what I've heard everybody hated Doctor Crow too. She was the one had her locked up in that room that night. '

' Doctor Crow was a woman?'

Charlie managed a giggle. ' She still is, I think. She's still alive.'

' Well, what's the mystery?' Jazz asked. ' If this Doctor locked her in, couldn't she have sneaked in during the night, unlocked the door, killed Hayley?' Jazz was working on her own theory.

' But why would she leave the knife, Jazz?' I asked her.

Again, Charlie shook her head. ' She had some kind of iron clad alibi. But the suspicion was always there. And...there's something else.'

' Wow, this story gets better by the minute.' Jazz moved closer to Charlie.

' When they found her in the morning, it looked as if she'd been in a terrible fight. She was bruised and battered and her face was all cut up. As if she'd been fighting for her life. And she hadn't been like that the night before either. Another mystery they didn't solve.'

' Is all this true?' I asked.

' I know, it sounds stranger than fiction, but I promise it's true.' Charlie blessed herself. ' Cross my heart and hope to die.'

' No wonder she haunts this place. She needs someone to find out the truth. ' Jazz looked around as if Hayley Brown might be standing somewhere between the gravestones, watching us. So did I. Expecting her white face to be staring at me, her voice pleading with me. ' Help me.'

Jazz squeezed my arm. 'She wants,' she paused '- somebody-' and she paused again,' to find out the truth.'

And that somebody was me, I thought. Hayley Brown, in her despair, had come to me. Her story, her mystery, already had me hooked.

' Will you be coming next week?' Charlie asked. 'I'll try to find out more about her.'

' Will you be here?' Jazz asked.

' I told you, I come every Saturday...I'm...I'm.. a volunteer .'

' Yeah, me and Tyler, we'll be back,' Jazz looked at me. ' Right Tyler?'

I didn't have to think about it. I knew I had to come back. I just didn't know what excuse we could make to get here again.

Charlie looked so pleased. She beamed a smile at us. She really did have such a pretty face. Then she came across and hugged me. ' I will look forward to that.' Then she whispered. ' and maybe together we'll solve the mystery of Hayley Brown.'

The bell rang then, sounding out plaintively in the dark afternoon. ' Lunch!' Jazz said. ' Come on, Charlie.'

Charlie held back. She held up the little bunch of flowers she had clutched in her hand.' One more grave to visit. I'll be with you in a minute.'

Jazz took my arm as we made our back to the house. ' This just gets better by the minute. Doesn't it? That's why you've been seeing her. She wants you to find out whodunit!' How excited she sounded, and I thought again, why hadn't this gift been bestowed on Jazz, who would love it? Why me?

One day, I was going to find that out.

The smell of chicken soup hit us as soon as we entered the kitchen. Annie pointed us to a seat. ' Sit down girls,'

Only two places had been laid at the table. ' Isn't Charlie eating with us?' I asked.

Annie let out one of her belly laughs. ' Charlie? You mean the lassie you were talking to in the garden?'

' She's just putting some flowers on a grave.' I said.

' What did Charlotte tell you,' Sister Phil came in then from the dining room.

' She's a volunteer, or a visitor, was it? She comes every Saturday.'

Annie laughed again. ' Charlie's here every Saturday, every day in fact.
'

' She's an inmate?' Jazz asked.

' We don't call them inmates, ' Sister Phil scolded.

Behind her Annie made a face.' It's like a hotel. We call them our guests.'

 I tried not to laugh.

' Was it a whole bunch of lies she told us?' Jazz asked.

' Charlotte has got a problem with the truth,' Sister Phil said.

' You mean, she tells lies?' I asked.

' All the time. She can't help it. But she never means any harm.'

' She has got another problem, Sister.' Annie said. ' I think you better tell them about that.'

Oh dear, what were we going to hear now?

' She is serial killer!' Jazz said. ' I knew it!'

Sister Phil hesitated. ' Not quite. Perhaps you should check your pockets to see if anything's missing.'

' She steals things?'

' Best wee pickpocket I've ever come across,' Annie said.

Jazz patted her pockets and shrugged. ' I'm fine.'

I checked mine. ' My phone's gone,' I said. And I remembered then how she had stumbled against me, and I had felt her hand against my jacket, but only thought she had been steadying herself.

' We'll get it back, don't worry.' Sister Phil assured us. ' She steals, but she never keeps anything.'

' See if she gives things back it makes her look good.' Annie said. ' She always says she found it, and when she gives it back she thinks that will make people like her. Wee soul,' she added with uncharacteristic sympathy.

' Oh thank you, Dr Annie,' Sister Phil said with a smile. ' But in a way, Annie's spot on.'

' I can't believe it. She seemed so normal.' Jazz said.

' Och, she is. She's not a bad girl. Not Charlie.' It seemed Annie liked her.

' We made arrangements to meet her here. Next week. ' I remembered.

After this revelation I expected the Sister Phil to say no. Instead, she smiled. 'Would you still be willing to do that? Come back, meet up with Charlotte?'

' And let her steal something else!' Jazz said. I put my hand on her arm. We had to come back, here was a perfect excuse.

' We wouldn't let that happen.' Sister Phil said. ' And a lot of the girls ignore Charlie. She's always so alone. It would be nice for her to have visitors, close to her own age.'

I didn't even have to ask Jazz what she would do. I knew what I was going to do. 'I'll come.'

' Oh well,' Jazz said. ' I'll come with you. But my pockets will be empty!'

CHAPTER 10

As we were leaving Sister Phil brought me my phone. ' Charlie says she found it on the ground. It must have dropped out of your pocket.' She sighed. ' She was just bringing it to you. It's what she always says.'

' Is that why she's here? Because she's a thief?' I asked.

' We never discuss why the girls are here. This is a fresh start for them.'

Charlie, and Hayley Brown were all we talked about on the way home.

' What do you think of that Charlie?' Jazz still couldn't get over how she'd stolen the phone. 'How did she do it? Did you feel her doing it? She must be a champion pickpocket? And she seemed so nice!'

' I got my phone back. And now at least we have an excuse to come back next week, and now we'll know what to expect from Charlie.'

' Do you think all that was the truth about Hayley Brown? I mean it's such a far fetched story. A locked room. Looking as if she'd been in a terrible fight, and a murder. A knife that wasn't there the night before. A doctor under suspicion. We fell for that hook line and sinker! First from Annie, then from Charlie. I wonder what the truth really is?'

But I knew someone who knew the truth-who wanted me to find that out. And I knew she would come back to tell me. So I was prepared for what happened that night...almost.

I was in the bathroom brushing my teeth, and I looked up and there in the mirror, standing behind me stood Hayley. Too close, right at my shoulder. Her face too white, her eyes too dark. I swivelled round, half expecting that there would be no one there in the bathroom, no one but me. The way it had been in dad's car.

But Hayley Brown was still there. I stepped back, and my toothbrush fell from my fingers and dropped to the floor. She always scared me, and I remembered in that second the stories about her, and what she had done. ' A malevolent ghost,' they had called her.

I waited for her to speak-to ask me to help her and I was ready with my answer. ' I'm trying, I am going to help you.'

But when she did speak it wasn't to ask for help. ' She told the truth.' There was a long pause. It was as if she was drawing up all the energy she had to say the words. A tap dripped in the shower, the only sound to break the silence. ' I was murdered.'

She closed her eyes, as if speaking had exhausted her.

' But how? You were in a locked room. How were you murdered?'

She moved even closer to me. Seemed to draw in another grave cold breath. 'Doctor Crow. Doctor Crow. You have to find her. '

There was a sudden banging on the bathroom door. It was Steven my brother. 'Tyler! Who have you got in there?'

'Nobody!' I shouted back. ' I was rehearsing a play.'

'Talking to yourself more like.' He laughed and moved away. ' As usual!'

I waited till I heard his room door close. I swung round, but Hayley was gone. Gone at least from the bathroom. But when I looked in the mirror above the sink. Her face was still there, staring at me.

' Help me!' she said again. And then the bathroom mist covered the mirror and swallowed her up.

CHAPTER 11

Monday at school and they were all waiting for me at the school gates. Jazz was there, already arguing with Adam. He shouted across to me as I approached them. 'Good thing this day release eh, Tyler.' Then he nudged Jazz. ' Though in her case it's care in the community.'

She pushed him back so hard he fell against Callum, and he in turn fell against Mac.

' I was just telling them about that Charlie,' Jazz said.

' She sounds wacko. I don't think you should go back,' Mac said.

He sounded as if he really cared, and I smiled.

Jazz grabbed my arm. ' Ignore them. Not in our league!' she was almost dragging me up the drive away from the boys. ' By the way, I found out about that Doctor Crow.' It amazed me the things Jazz could find out. She was better than a detective. ' Still lives near here. I've even got her address. Her life fell apart after the Hayley Brown incident. There was no evidence against her, just that it was her knife they found, and she didn't know how Hayley got it. But the suspicion was always there, that she had been involved in her death someway. '

' Why do you want to know about this Doctor Crow? And who is this Hayley Brown?'

It was Mac, coming up behind us. Jazz thinks faster than me, no doubt about that. She answered Mac without a blush. ' Me and Tyler heard about them at Bonaventure House. Hayley Brown was murdered, locked room mystery, and Doctor Crow got the blame. Is that not a fantastic story!'

'Trust Tyler to find a story!' he laughed, then, almost satisfied, he hurried off after Adam.

I waited till Mac, and the rest were out of earshot. I whispered to Jazz. ' I've got to go and see this Doctor Crow.'

Jazz rolled her eyes. ' You are off your chump. This doctor could be a murderer. Probably is...and you want to go and see her?'

Jazz was the only one I could explain things to. ' That's what Hayley wants me to do, Jazz.'

' You saw her again!' I could see her tremble with excitement. ' Well, you're not going alone. I'll be your bodyguard.' She pulled me against her. ' We are a great team!'

CHAPTER 12

It would be the following Sunday before we would be able to go to see this Doctor Crow. I hoped Hayley Brown would understand. When you're my age you can't just jump in your car and drive in hot pursuit of someone, take time off school to follow suspects, and I've got to be in by ten. My mum and dad expect to know where I'm going and who with, and I've got to have money for busses and trains. Not easy this being a psychic detective at my age.

I had a feeling Hayley Brown didn't understand that. She would not let me be. She appeared everywhere. She stood in the classroom watching me with those soulful eyes. I couldn't get away from her. It's hard to concentrate on lessons when someone is staring at you, especially when that someone is a ghost. Someone no one else can see. She never moved. She simply stood in the corner and stared .

On the way home from school she would be waiting at the bus stop, standing in the queue along with everyone else. Normally when I saw the dead, they looked just as alive as you or me. But Hayley Brown looked like a ghost. She was grey and almost transparent. The nightdress she wore had once been white, now it was stained with blood and it was dirty and torn. Her hair, though you could still see it was fair, was lank and greasy as if it hadn't been washed for a long time. It was as if she needed me to see her as she was when she had died.

She must be desperate for my help, appearing so often, appearing everywhere, saying nothing. Why?

Hayley wanted me to find out the truth about Dr. Crow. Had this doctor got away with murder? Where had that knife come from? And she wanted me to find out quickly. Almost as if there was a deadline, some kind of race against time. And I remembered the date on her tombstone. **November 27th.**

That was only three weeks from now. Was that the reason? She needed me to change things before then.

Jazz was looking forward to seeing this doctor too. Doing her detective thing always appealed to her. She had found out Doctor's Crow's address. She had even worked out what we would say when we met her.

' We'll tell her it's for our project, Trapped. We've been to Bonaventure House, and they have agreed we can do it, and we hoped she could help us too.'

' Her career was ruined in Bonaventure House.' I reminded her. ' She might not want to talk about it. She won't even let us in.'

' All you might need is a few words with her, at the doorstep. You'll get a feeling, You will sense something. I know you will.' Jazz was that sure of my gift!

' You're brilliant, Jazz. I couldn't do any of these things without you.'

' My mum thinks you're a good influence on me,' she told me.

That made me laugh. ' It's you that's the good influence on me.' And it was true. How my life had changed since I'd met her, and all my other friends. This 'gift', this special gift I had, it had blossomed since I came to St. Anthony's and I sometimes wondered if Jazz was a big part of that. That she might have been the catalyst for everything.

As we had promised, on that next Saturday, we took the bus again to Bonaventure House to see Charlie.

' Check your pockets before you go in,' Jazz said as we stepped off the bus. ' I made sure mine are empty.'

This time we arrived at the same time as lots of other visitors. Older couples, come to visit a wayward daughter, women on their own, or with children. There were boyfriends too. Each of them with a story to tell about the girl they were coming to visit. We followed them to the visiting area in the new glass walled extension. The visiting area was all very plush , with soft sofas, and thick rugs and tables and chairs and even a little cafe. For the first time we saw other girls. Some of them looked scary, tough and hard, and it made me wonder how I would feel if I had been sent here, locked in. If I had come here on my own, knowing no one, trusting no one. Would I pretend to be as tough as these other girls? To prove I was afraid of nothing? To make them think, perhaps, that they should be afraid of me? Is that what they were doing, pretending to be so tough? Or would I be so scared of them I couldn't hide it?

I was so glad I had a lovely family, a safe home, friends. So many here didn't, and never had.

Charlie was waiting for us, fidgeting at a table, on her own. She jumped up with excitement when she saw us. ' Oh you came, you came! I knew you would.'

She threw her arms around us as if we were her best friends. ' Did you get your phone back, Tyler?' she didn't wait for my answer. ' You must have dropped it. Lucky I found it, and her voice became soft.' And not one of those other girls. You might not have got it back.' She nodded across to a hard looking blonde girl, the roots of her hair black as coal. She was sitting slouched at another table, deliberately not talking to a drab woman sitting at the table with her. ' That's Babs. She's dangerous,' Charlie went on. 'She's another Hayley Brown. I heard them saying that. She's almost as bad as she was.'

' Born bad,' Jazz said softly.

' Although, I suppose you can't blame Hayley Brown completely, if you knew her background,' Charlie said. ' She came from the most awful family.   She had to be taken away from them when she was just a baby...and, do you know, she was almost adopted by the loveliest couple. They adored her. And then....'

There was a long pause. ' And then, what, Charlie?' I asked.

'It's an awful story. The day before they were due to take her with them, the day before the adoption papers were to be signed.... there was this terrible accident. Just as the couple were driving out of the gates a runaway lorry crashed into them. They were killed instantly.'   Charlie's voice broke a little.

Even Jazz was affected. ' But that's terrible!'

Charlie nodded. ' I know. Tragic.'

' And what happened to Hayley after that?' I asked her.

' She was sent back to her awful family,' Charlie said. ' They neglected her, she was abused, so she kept being taken away from them. And what was worse, being sent back. She was in and out of care, no one really bothered about what happened to her.' Her pretty face screwed up. ' Can you blame her turning out like she did? No wonder she was bad.' She snapped it out.

And, she was right, who could blame Hayley Brown for what she had become after all that?

CHAPTER 13

Out of the glass front of the visiting area where we sat, I could see that isolated little house. The high stained glass windows, the chimney, the grey stone walls. It seemed as if the house was waiting for me, calling for me. It chilled me just looking at that house. It made me afraid. Was that how it made Hayley feel when she was dragged into it? Was I feeling her fear?

' I need a breath of air,' I said, and I stood up. Jazz and Charlie did too.

' Are you okay?' Jazz asked. ' Do you want to go a walk?'

I didn't want company. I needed to be alone. But I knew I looked as pale as I felt. Jazz wouldn't leave me. So we all left together and we went outside. A wind came up, it shivered through the trees, and it grew cold. I drew my jacket closed around me. The sky was all at once heavy with grey clouds. They raced across the sky. I looked around. Jazz and Charlie were no longer there walking behind me. I was alone.

I knew what had happened. It had happened so often to me. They were in another time. In the now. I was in the past. Hayley Brown's past.

I turned quickly when I heard the screams. A door in the main house opened, and Hayley ran out. I'd never seen her like this. I'd never seen her alive. Her dark blonde hair was flying around her face, her eyes wide and angry. She looked like someone wild.

' I'm not an animal!' she was yelling at someone I couldn't see. Someone who was still inside the house. ' Leave me be!'

Just then a woman ran out behind her and grabbed her by the arm. A woman, her hair black as night, drawn back into a tight bun at the back of her head.

' You're coming with me!' she shouted. ' I've had enough of you.'

The woman was breathing so hard I could hardly make out her words. She was trying so hard to control Hayley Brown. Hayley swung around, she grabbed a hold of the woman's hair and pulled. She pulled so hard the woman's head was yanked back almost to the ground. The bun came loose, and great trails of jet black hair flew out. I could see pain and anger on the woman's face. Then, all at once, she jerked herself free. Now she twisted round and she grabbed Hayley's arm even tighter, she turned her round, locked both her arms behind her. Hayley still had clumps of the woman's thick black hair in her fingers. But now, it was clear the woman was in charge. She had regained control. She began to march Hayley in front of her, almost lifting her off the ground. They were coming towards me, heading for the small house. Hayley could hardly keep her feet.

Hayley's face was streaked with tears, but they were tears of anger, frustration. ' I hate you, Crow!' she yelled, her words squeezed through her gritted teeth, her voice filled with defiance. ' I'll get you back for this!'

So this was Doctor Crow.

And equally defiant, this woman, this Doctor Crow said. ' Feeling's mutual, Miss Brown.'

As they came closer Hayley struggled even more. ' Don't put me in there!'

Doctor Crow didn't break her stride. 'It's your own fault. We can't trust you with the others. You're given chance after chance. You only get what you deserve.'

And Hayley screamed again. ' Don't put me in there!' She tried to kick at the doctor, but though Hayley Brown was strong, this Doctor Crow was stronger. She pushed her ahead. And I could only watch as they passed right by me without a glance. For them I wasn't there. I watched Hayley being forced up the steps to the front door, struggling against every step. I watched her as she was pushed inside, still screaming. The door slammed shut. I waited, and I could still hear Hayley's screams. She was swearing now, vowing vengeance on the doctor for what she was doing. And then, all at once, the screaming, the swearing stopped. She was quiet. I imagined them giving her some kind of injection, something to calm her. Was I meant to follow her inside, help her now? But I couldn't move, because I was so afraid. Afraid to go into that isolated house again. Was that because it scared Hayley so much, or was there some other reason? Something else I should be afraid of?

I turned to look back to the main house. At almost every window girls were watching, their faces impassive, not one glimmer of sympathy in their eyes.

And then in a shimmer of light they were gone. It grew warmer. I heard Jazz calling me. She was standing with Charlie. ' Tyler! You're off in one of your dreams again. Come on! We're going for a walk!'

CHAPTER 14

'I have to see this Doctor Crow, Jazz,' I said as we were leaving that day. Charlie had asked us to come back the following Saturday, almost begged us. She seemed to have forgotten that she had told us she was not an inmate but a visitor. I had immediately said yes. Even before Jazz had a chance to speak. Whatever I had to do for Hayley, it had to be done here, at Bonaventure House.

' Of course, I'll come,' Jazz said. ' But you know just because someone's dead doesn't mean they're good. If she was so bad in life well.....' Jazz shrugged as if...do I need to say more? I knew that was worrying her. It worried me too.

' No one's born bad, Jazz.' Surely that was true. ' And she had such a horrible upbringing. She could have been with a lovely family who cared for her, except for that awful accident. Instead, no one wanted her. I feel so sorry for her. We are so lucky, Jazz. It could be us in there.'

Jazz shivered. ' Don't even want to think about that. I couldn't bear it, Tyler. To be locked away. Stuck in that place with all of them. And let's face it, some of those girls are scary.'

' No wonder Charlie lives in her dream world. Trying to pretend she's only a visitor.'

' I wish we could help her,' Jazz said.

'I think we are, just by coming to see her. That seems to mean a lot to her.'

Jazz linked her arm in mine. ' So what happened today?' She didn't even wait for an answer. 'You saw her, didn't you? I saw you were in one of your dreams, and I thought. She's seeing something I can't see.' She giggled, loving it. ' What happened? Tell me.'

Was I confiding in Jazz too much? I had done it before and put her in danger. But surely there was no danger this time. And she would forget everything when I changed things for Hayley Brown. When I changed time. When I put things back the way they were meant to be. And it was so good having someone to talk it over with. This was such a lonely gift I had been given. ' I saw her being dragged into that house...that isolated house. She was screaming, Jazz. She didn't want to go. And it was this Doctor Crow who was dragging her there.'

Jazz loved that. She punched the air. ' Evil doctor. Seen it a million times in movies. You have got to go see this Doctor Crow then.'

' I still wonder if she will even talk to us when we mention Bonaventure House. '

Jazz was thinking fast. ' What about this then? We walk past her house. I pretend to trip. Fall flat on my face. You have to run in to her, beg her for help. You think I'm concussed or something. She's a doctor, she'd have to let us in, help us. Hippocratic Oath and all that.'

' If she had any sense she would send us packing.'

' Here's another idea.' Jazz was really warming up now. ' We could pretend to be collecting for Bonaventure House.. When she opens the door, we say...oh, are you the same Doctor Crow who used to work at

Bonaventure House? Isn't that a coincidence...and once we're inside we throw Hayley Brown into the conversation.'

I laughed. ' Then she'd be likely to throw us out. Honestly Jazz, how do you come up with these things.'

' Watch a lot of tv,' she said.

' Why don't we stick to our original plan. Tell her the same story we told them at Bonaventure House. '

Jazz sighed. ' Not very dramatic. Not using my acting skills at all. But never mind, it's worth a try.'

That night, I was in the bathroom brushing my teeth when she came. Once again, appearing behind me in the mirror above the sink. ' Her face grey, her eyes black holes in her face. ' Help Me.'

The words came from somewhere deep inside her. Why couldn't she leave me alone? I was doing my best. I yelled an answer. ' I'm helping you, Hayley! You must see that.'

My mum banged on the door. ' You okay in there!'

' Sorry mum, it was nothing.' And when I looked again, Hayley Brown had gone.   She was growing impatient. She was desperate. Growing more desperate by the moment.

I understood. I was desperate too.

Desperate for it to be over.

CHAPTER 15

' The name says it all, doesn't it? Crow. Perfect name for a murderer,' Jazz said as we made our way up the street to Dr Crow's house. ' I wonder what she looks like?'

But I knew what she looked like. I had seen her. Her black hair pulled loose by Hayley Brown, the anger in her face. She would be older now. Fifteen years older. I wondered if she'd changed much.

I had never been in this village, just a few miles out of town. A few houses, a church, a pub and that was it. Blink and you would miss it. I was surprised Doctor Crow still lived in the area, especially after the publicity there had been because of the death of Hayley Brown. Was that the sign of a clear conscience, or no conscience at all? Her house was on the main street, the only street in fact, in the middle of a line of stone built houses. There were boxes with faded summer flowers on the window sill. The front door was painted green, but it was badly in need of a paint job. The brass nameplate needed polishing too.

CROW.

Jazz looked at me. ' Are you ready for this?'

I nodded. I would have to be. If I was going to help Hayley, I had to see this Doctor Crow.

I would never have recognised the woman who opened the door. The black hair was streaked with grey, and it lay in long unkempt strands on her shoulders. Her skin was clear, but there was something in her eyes that it took me a minute to recognise. Exhaustion, or despair, I wasn't sure which. ' Dr. Crow?' I asked.

' Can I help you?'

It was Jazz who answered her, rattling out her words almost in a single breath. ' I hope you don't think we've got a cheek on us, but you see me and Tyler here,' she paused and pushed me forward. 'This is Tyler. I'm Jazz, well we're doing a project in school. It's called Trapped. We've to research and write something with that as the theme... and we've decided to write about girls in care... because you don't get more trapped than that.. and we've been to Bonaventure House...' As soon as she spoke the name I saw suspicion in the doctor's eyes . 'And they're really happy for us to do that, because we only want to write nice things, and they thought it would be good if we could talk to you. Everybody at the Bonaventure talks so highly of you...it's Dr. Crow this, and Dr. Crow that... and if you want to talk to someone who knows, you have to talk to Doctor Crow... that's what they said.'

My mouth just hung open listening to Jazz. How did she come up with these things?

' We don't want to intrude but you worked with children in care for a long time, we thought you could add a little to what we know already.' I could hear my voice tremble.

' You looking for gossip?' she said.' Well, you will get none from me.'
Her voice was harsh.

' No, please...'

She began to close the door on us before I could assure her we
weren't, but just then an old lady came hobbling down the hall calling out to
us. ' Who's that? Oh, is that your friends? I knew they'd come today. Come
on in, my dears. Let them in now.' She waved us to come inside, but Doctor
Crow still kept closing the door.

' Mother, go back in the living room. These are not my friends.'

But the woman never stopped hobbling closer, waving that away with
her cane. ' Emily, my dear, don't keep your friends at the door. They've
come a long way.' She pushed Dr. Crow aside, and next thing Jazz and I
were being pulled inside the house. Dr. Crow let out a long sigh.

' You don't have too many friends, Emily, you can't risk losing these.' I
looked at Jazz and raised an eyebrow. We could not believe what was
happening. We were practically dragged into the living room by this old
lady. I tried to murmur an apology to Dr. Crow, but she only stood back
with her arms folded, her face grim.

' Now, sit yourself down. You must have some tea. Would you like some tea?' the old lady asked.

' No, they don't want tea, mother. They have to go.'

' Of course they want tea. Who brought you up? It's only good manners.'

I shook my head, burning with embarrassment, not so the bold Jazz. ' Tea would be lovely,' she said.

' Emily will get us some, won't you Emily?' Her daughter still stood in the doorway, unsmiling. I didn't blame her.

'Oh never mind, I'll get it myself. Honestly, Emily! You can be so rude at times.' And Mrs. Crow waddled into the kitchen.

' I'm so sorry, we didn't mean....' I tried hard to apologise.

Her hard face softened for a moment. ' Not your fault. As you can see, my mother is a force to be reckoned with.'

' Hurricane Crow,' Jazz giggled and it even brought the semblance of a smile to the doctor's face.

' Exactly,' she said.

' Do you want us to go now?' I backed towards the door. Jazz stayed sitting.

Doctor Crow let out a sigh and sat across from her. ' No point. You're in now. 'She pointed me to a seat. ' What kind of piece are you intending to write.'

'Nothing controversial, we promise.' I said.

' If you've been to Bonaventure House then there is no use pretending you don't know about what happened there.'

I blurted out. ' But that's not what we're interested in.' I blushed to my roots. I am just not a good liar.

Without a doubt Jazz is.   ' We just want a few positive quotes. Bonaventure House has had such a bad press. We wanted to write something nice about the work that's done there.'

' This is all I am saying then.' The doctor took a deep breath before she began.' I loved working at Bonaventure House. It was very rewarding. I loved the girls there....most of them, they were girls who had had bad starts with families, or sometimes with none. Girls whose lives had been hard. At Bonaventure we did our best to make those lives better.'

' Bad girls, my mum said they used to be called.'

Dr. Crow shook her head. ' No, not fair. Very few people are born bad.'

Born bad, there was that phrase again. ' Very few?' I asked. ' You mean there are some who are born bad?'

' Like that Hayley Brown,' Jazz said.

Dr. Crow's whole body stiffened. ' I think I made it clear I am not dishing out any gossip. I am not talking about that girl.'

She didn't stop Jazz. ' The girls who are there now say she even haunts the place.'

I tried to sound as natural as Jazz. ' Some of the girls told us stories about her, they said some people have seen her, in the night. In that house....'

' Where she died.' Jazz finished for me.

' So now, it's ghost stories you're looking for,' Doctor Crow said.

Would Dr. Crow have said more then? I don't know. Just at that Mrs. Crow came bustling in with a tray. On it were a teapot and teacups and saucers. ' Here we are,' she said cheerily.

She placed the tray on the coffee table and began pouring from the teapot. Nothing came out. I looked at Dr. Crow, she only raised an eyebrow. Mrs Crow handed Jazz an empty cup.

' Oh thank you,' Jazz said, and she began sipping from the cup. ' Lovely tea.'

No wonder I like Jazz so much. She drank from that cup as if it was filled to the brim with Earl Grey.

' Oh, you like my jasmine tea then?'

Jazz spluttered and laughed. ' Jasmine tea!   Now there's a coincidence. That's my name, Jasmine. But everyone calls me Jazz.'

That was when I realised we hadn't even properly introduced ourselves. ' Oh, I am sorry. She's Jazz and I'm Tyler. Tyler Lawless.'

' Tyler....Lawless?' Dr. Crow asked. Her cup rattled in her saucer. Her face went white.

' Is everything okay?' I asked.

' No, no....' she looked puzzled. ' Look, I think you'd better leave now.' She stood up. Our cue to go.

Jazz and I stood up too. ' Thank you for the tea, Mrs. Crow.'

The old lady clasped my hand and Jazz's. ' Come again, don't be a stranger.'

At the front door I apologised to Dr. Crow again. ' We didn't mean to cause any trouble.'

Dr. Crow's face was impassive. ' I do not want you to write anything about me in your article. Do not mention my name. You can say a source informed you of the good work done in Bonaventure House for these girls. How difficult these girls' backgrounds have been. But nothing else. Nothing. Do you understand? And nothing about Hayley Brown. I said very few were born bad, well, Hayley Brown was born bad. She was bad when she was alive, and she is still bad. Even in death. She ruined my life, my career. But if you put that in any article I will sue you.' Then she slammed the front door shut.

We both looked back at the house as we walked up the street. Dr. Crow was at a window, she looked like a ghost herself. Her face so white, her grey hair hanging on her shoulders. She wasn't smiling.

Jazz tucked her arm in mine. ' What was that all about? Did you see her face when she heard your name?'

' That was strange, wasn't it?'

Jazz shivered. 'Don't tell me she's not weird.'

CHAPTER 16

I didn't know what I had achieved by seeing Doctor Crow. I had had no feelings when I met her, I had learned nothing. Why had Hayley wanted me to find her so badly? Yet, the doctor had looked at me so strangely when she heard my name. I couldn't understand why. It was all clear to Jazz.

' She is definitely responsible for Hayley Brown's death. Definitely. Did you see the guilt written all over her face.'

' I thought she looked desperate. Her career ruined, her life ruined. Come on, Jazz. And it must be hard for her looking after her mother.'

' None of the girls liked her, Charlie told us. She seemed to be universally unpopular!'

' She did have Hayley to contend with.' I said.

' Hayley Brown, look at the background she had. No wonder she turned out bad. Poor Hayley.'

That made me laugh. ' When did you start feeling sorry for her?'

' Don't you? I mean, you're the one she's haunting.' She grinned. ' You tell her what I said the next time you see her. Tell her, I'm beginning to understand what she was going through!'

Hayley was all I thought about. Was I meant to save her? Or to bring her murderer to justice? And was that murderer really Doctor Crow? I kept waiting for her to appear and tell me. And she didn't, and that surprised me too. All the week after our visit to Doctor Crow I saw nothing of Hayley Brown.

We went back to Bonaventure House the next Saturday. Charlie was waiting for us at the gates. Her face beamed with pleasure. ' You came again...you're just wonderful, both of you.'

I watched for a sign that Hayley was there, as we sat in the visiting area, as we walked through the gardens. Jazz kept glancing at me, and I kept shaking my head. Nothing. We went back into the warmth of the visiting area and I sat, staring ahead, not joining in the conversation. I was waiting for something to happen. I was waiting for Hayley Brown.

' Is anything wrong, Tyler?' Charlie asked me.

' No, no, just a bit...bit of a headache.' I stood up. ' Maybe I'll go to the loo, splash my face.'

Jazz stood up with me. ' I'll come with you.'

I pushed her back into her seat. ' I'll be back in a minute. I'm fine, honest.'

I went to the toilets and stared into the mirror above the sink for a long time, waiting. Waiting for Hayley Brown to appear.

But she didn't.

It was only when I came out of the toilets and looked across the lawn to the old house that I knew she was here.

The door was lying open.

I looked around, other girls were lounging on sofas, talking to their visitors, but no one was watching me. Jazz and Charlie were absorbed in a shared magazine. No one else seemed to see I was even there. I pushed through the glass doors and began walking towards the house.

The house was always locked up, wasn't it? Perhaps today someone was inside, brushing it out, cleaning it.

But I knew that the door was open, especially for me. Only for me.

I crossed the lawn leading to the house, walked up the path. A chill wind was blowing up from the river. Still no one seemed to notice me. I knew why. I was in that halfway place between the past and the present. I stood in the doorway. There was no sound or sign of anyone inside. The corridor ahead of me was dark, the shutters closed. I looked around again. No one was looking my way, or interested in what I was doing. In fact, standing here in the doorway, I was hidden from view. No one could even have seen me.

Don't go in.

Who was warning me? Was that my voice?

Don't go in.

I so wanted to take that advice. But it was too late. I couldn't have stopped myself.

I stepped inside.

Was I in her time, or mine? I couldn't be sure.

What made it so chilly in here? Was it the presence of Hayley, long dead, waiting?

' Is anyone here?' My voice echoed through the house. I imagined it like a finger of ghostly mist floating along the corridor, in and out of the rooms. There was no answer.

I took another step into the hall, and then another, until I was standing in the living room. I turned and looked along the corridor towards Room 4. The room where she had died. I moved closer, step by step, the only sound was my footsteps on the wooden floor. My eyes were locked on the door of that room and as I stared, it swung slowly open.

I kept walking. Perhaps now was the time when I would witness her dying moments, I would see at last who was responsible for her death. I would save her. I would change the past, or put it back the way it was meant to be.

Another step.

And Hayley Brown stepped out of the room, holding out her hands to me, those scars livid white against her skin.

'Come to me, Tyler,' she whispered. ' Come to me.' And she beckoned me forward with those outstretched hands and then she stepped back into the room.

I was afraid, I had never been so afraid. I reached the doorway and stopped. Hayley was waiting inside and for the first time there was a strange, satisfied smile on her face. I was here at last.

' Come to me, Tyler,' she whispered.

One more step and I would be inside the room with her.

CHAPTER 18

There was a sudden piercing scream from outside, followed by shouts of anger. Something was happening out there. I swung round. I could hear Jazz yelling. ' Leave her!'

I looked back at Hayley. Her eyes were wild. She was shaking her head frantically, her fingers reaching out to me like claws. ' Help me!!!' she screamed it too.

For a split second I didn't know what to do, then I heard Jazz again. ' Get off her!'

She sounded desperate. Between Hayley Brown and Jazz there was no choice. Jazz would always come first. I'd come back. But Jazz needed me in the here and now. Hayley would have to wait.

I ran out of the house. Two girls were rolling about on the ground outside the visiting room. One of them was Charlie. Jazz was doing her best to separate them, but I could see that the other girl had a grip of Charlie's hair and wouldn't let go. I saw at once this was Babs, the scary one Charlie had pointed out to us. In fact, just as I reached them this Babs lunged out at Jazz and grabbed her too, dragging her to the ground.

Jazz jumped to her feet, but she was ready to leap back in and begin fighting herself. I grabbed her and held her back.

' What happened here?'

Jazz was breathless. ' That Babs jumped Charlie. She just lifted her off her seat and began punching her. Chased her out here.'

Another girl beside us swung Jazz round. ' Babs is my mate. Charlie stole her purse. That's all she ever does. Steal things!'

I tried to pull Charlie free. ' Let her go.' I yelled to Babs.

Between us Jazz and I managed to help Charlie to her feet. Babs was held back by some of the other girls. She looked wild and scary. ' That's the last time you steal anything from me.'

I felt Charlie tremble beside me. ' I didn't steal it. I found it.' She reached into her pocket. Her hands were shaking. ' Here, I was going to give it to you.' She threw a colourful bulging purse at the girl. 'Check it. There's nothing missing.'

The purse landed at the other girl's feet. She bent and picked it up. ' Better not be,' she sneered. ' Cause you cannot get away from me in here. Just remember that, Charlie. You cannot get away from me...or my mates.'

The way she said it scared me. Charlie's whole body was shaking, and no wonder. There was a viciousness in the way Babs was looking at her. Charlie moved closer to me and Jazz as if she needed our protection.

Just then Sister Phil came running up. 'What on earth is going on here?'

' She's been at her stealing again,' Babs said, poking a finger towards Charlie.

' I found the purse. I told you that.' Charlie's voice shook. She looked at Sister Phil. ' I gave it back.'

Sister Phil sighed. ' Oh Charlie,' was all she said.

I wanted to shout to her. Tell her that this Babs had threatened Charlie. I wanted her to know that she said she's going to get her. But I knew that would probably only make things worse for Charlie. Instead I slipped my arm round Charlie's shaking shoulders and pulled her close.

' I'll speak to both of you in the office.' Sister Phil said.

She strode off, ordering the girls to follow her, so she didn't see the backward glance Babs shot at Charlie which was a threat in itself. As soon as she was out of sight Charlie burst into tears.

' Tell Sister Phil what she said, Charlie. They'll protect you.'

Charlie shook her head. ' And be a grass? That would only make things worse. You've got to be joking. Anyway, they can't protect you all the time. Not in here. I'll be alone sometimes, and that's when she'll get me.' She looked from me to Jazz. ' I didn't steal her purse. I did find it. Honest.'

Did she believe that herself, I wondered? She seemed to believe all her other lies.

She clutched at my jacket. ' Can I come home with you?'

I felt tears nipping my eyes. ' I wish you could, Charlie.' I said, and I meant it. I hated leaving her here.

' Why can't I? I could just walk out the gate with you. No one would notice. Please don't make me stay here. I hate it here.'

Just then Sister Phil appeared again and called Charlie. ' I'm waiting, Charlie.'

Still, Charlie clutched at me. ' Help me.'

And I thought, here was Charlie, alive, needing my help, and I didn't know how to help her. I seemed only able to help the dead.

' When we come next week, we'll go out somewhere.' Jazz promised her. ' We'll ask if that's okay.' Jazz was near to tears too.

Charlie shook her head. ' It'll be too late. She'll get me before that. Let me come with you now! Please!'

Sister Phil called again. 'Charlie!'

' We'll go with you now,' I said. ' We'll tell Sister Phil that Babs threatened you. You won't get the blame for grassing.'

Now both Jazz and I were crying too.

Charlie pushed us away from her. ' No. That'll only make it worse. Can't you understand! ' Now she was sobbing. ' I hate it here. I'd do anything to get out of here. I wish I was dead.'

And she ran from us, heading away from Sister Phil. She disappeared round the corner of the big house before we could even move. Sister Phil called her again, then she ran after her.

CHAPTER 20

We called Bonaventure House every day that week. We wanted to make sure Charlie was all right. Let her know we hadn't forgotten about her. We only got to speak to her once. On the Wednesday, when she said very calmly everything was okay. I told Jazz I had a feeling she had been told to say that so as not to worry us.

' We'll see you Saturday, okay?' I told her.

' You don't have to,' she said. Her voice was flat and unemotional.

' Of course we will.' I waited for an answer but none came. 'You're sure everything's okay, Charlie.'

But no matter how many times we asked her, the answer was the same. She was fine.

And as if Charlie wasn't enough for me to worry about, I had Hayley Brown too. Every day, I would see her, somewhere, on the edge of my vision. I would turn and she wouldn't be there. Or, I would almost catch a glimpse of a faint image of her in a dark corner of my room. Just standing, watching me. Always, she had that same desperate look about her. It was as if it was taking so much of her strength to come to me, but that strength would only last for so long. Time was running out for her. November 27th was less than two weeks away.

Whatever had to be done for her, I had to do it on Saturday. I had to go back into that house and face her. I had to find out the truth about her death.

Sister Phil was waiting for us when we arrived at Bonaventure House that Saturday. ' I can't let you take Charlie out today,' she said. 'Not the way she's feeling.'

' But we promised her,' Jazz said.

' If she went out today, goodness knows where she would go. What she would do. She'd slip away from you. We've been very worried about her.'

' But we promised her,' Jazz said again.

' I've already told her. She understands. And I think it's safer if she stays here.'

' What do you mean? Safer?'

But she didn't have to tell me. I knew what she meant. They were afraid she might do something stupid, that if they let her out of their sight, she might try to kill herself. Suicide watch. That horrible phrase leapt into my mind.

' She's terrified of this Babs,' Jazz said.

' We've kept her well away from Babs. Charlie's in a room by herself, and she can lock the door.'

Yes, I thought, well away from any physical harm. No one has touched her, or hurt her, but I'd bet inside she wasn't fine. Inside she'd still be terrified.

' Can't you get a hold of that mother of hers?' Jazz asked.

' You mean, the film star? Or the rock singer?' she smiled. ' Don't believe anything Charlie tells you. She's always making up stories.'

But Charlie hadn't told us her mother was a film star or a rock singer. She had told us that her mother was a decent woman and she had let her down with all the trouble she had gotten herself into. I wondered what the real truth was about Charlie.

' Can we still visit her today?'

' Oh yes, she's looking forward to that.'

' Poor Charlie,' I whispered to Jazz, as we headed to the visiting area.

' I wish I could adopt her,' Jazz said.

' Me too. We've got to find some way to help her. There has to be something we can do.'

Charlie was waiting for us at the door. She looked pale but her eyes brightened when she saw us come in. ' I'm so sorry we can't go out,' she said at once. ' Hated to disappoint you, but there's just so much to do here. I wouldn't have time. Maybe next week.'

She had convinced herself it had been her decision. Nothing wrong with that, I thought. Her lies protected her from the truth that would hurt too much. 'Yes, definitely next week,' I said.

Jazz reached out and touched her hand. 'No trouble from....you know who?'

We glanced inside the waiting room and could see Babs slouched in a chair, wrapped in viciousness.

'Babs? No. She knew I hadn't taken her purse. She apologised to me eventually.' Charlie laughed, but I noticed a bruise on her cheek. How had she got it? I didn't dare ask. She had convinced herself of this lie, another lie. I couldn't let her know we didn't believe it.

We were both just relieved that Charlie seemed better. We sat in the visiting area and had coke and crisps and talked and Jazz had us laughing telling Charlie about our friends.

'See when we take you out for the day next week, you're going to meet them. There's Callum, he's a bit of a nerd, but he is so nice. Everybody likes Callum. Right, Tyler?'

I smiled. Glad to see Charlie smiling too.

' But you can't have him as your boyfriend. He's taken. Aisha and him are like that.' Jazz crossed one finger over the other. '   I don't know what she sees in him.' Then she giggled. ' and wait till you meet Mac and Adam.'

' Oh they all sound lovely. I'm dying to meet them.'

' Mac's taken too.' She nodded her head towards me. 'He's Tyler's.'

' So what about this Adam?' Charlie asked.

' Oh I wouldn't wish him on my worst enemy. No, we'll get somebody much better for you.'

She gave me a nudge. ' What about your brother, Tyler. Steven's a bit dishy?'

It always amazed me how so many of my friends thought my brother was good looking. ' Maybe once she sees him she won't think he's so dishy!'

I let Jazz do all the talking, and I listened and her voice grew faint and the sounds in the room seemed to fade. It was as if a veil had dropped over the room, and I was on one side of it, and everyone else was on the other.

 I looked out of the window across the gardens and the door of the old house was lying open.

And Hayley Brown was standing at the entrance, waiting.

CHAPTER 21

' I'm going outside for a bit,' I said. Even my own voice sounded distant. I was moving already into another time. Jazz looked up. Did she know by my face that something was happening?

' Want company?'

I shook my head, and she gave me a nod. She understood. I looked out towards the old house, and she was still standing in shadow. Hayley Brown. Jazz followed my gaze. I knew she saw nothing. But she sensed she was there.

' Go,' Jazz said. ' Get this over with.'

My heart was beating like a drum as I left the cafe and made my way to the old house. The door still lay open, but Hayley was no longer there. People walked past me. Did they see an open door too? I bet they didn't. To them the door was still locked tight. It was only for me that door lay open.

I was in that never land, between then and now.

I stood at the doorway, afraid to move further, but there was no going back now. Today was the day I was meant to change things for Hayley. I only took one step inside and the air grew immediately chill. Ghostly cold, I thought, though the day was warm for November. My footsteps made no sound on the wooden floor, as I walked up the hall. All I could hear was my own frightened breathing. I stood in the living room and turned down the hallway to the bedrooms, and even though I was expecting to see her, I was still taken by surprise when Hayley stepped from the open door of room 4.

Dead as dead, in that once white gown, and with that pale grey face. She beckoned me forward with her bloodstained fingers, her long nails encrusted with blood. She moved inside the room, as if she was floating. Her eyes never left me, locking me in, making sure my nerve wouldn't fail me. Hayley Brown needed me to be in that room. Was that so I could see the moment of her death? So that I could stop her from dying? Stop Doctor

Crow from killing her? Or just so at last I could solve the mystery of what had actually happened that night long ago.

What kept me walking on was the thought that I could put things back the way they were meant to be. If I could change things, Hayley would live and Doctor Crow would not be a murderer. A happy ending all round. That thought was what gave me the courage to keep moving.

My teeth began to chatter. I couldn't stop them. My feet were reluctant to move at all. At last I was there at the doorway.

Room. 4. Hayley stood inside, holding her arms out to me. Welcoming me in.

' What is it you want me to do, Hayley. What is it you want me to see?'

She didn't answer. I took one step into the room and everything around me rippled and changed. The room was no longer bare. There was a bed in the corner, with a bright green cover, beside it, there was a table with a reading lamp. There was a wooden chair, and a desk. I knew then I was back in her time. And Hayley herself, she became more solid, more real, yet not real, because I was the ghost now as I always was when I moved into the past. It was as if our two times had fused. I was almost in hers, she was almost in mine.

She came toward me, her arms held wide. She was smiling. ' You're here at last,' she said softly. 'I thought you'd never come.'

She wanted to hug me, to thank me. And of course she couldn't. She couldn't hug a ghost. I would be smoke to her. She would be only mist to me. She would pass through me. But I didn't want her to even try. She was too close and I was afraid.

I took a step back. Don't be afraid, Tyler, I told myself. Nothing can hurt you here. But an embrace from a dead girl frightened me. I didn't want it. I tried to take another step back, but it was as if my feet were glued to the floor. I could not move.

' Thank you, Tyler,' her voice a whisper almost against my ear. ' Thank you.'

I closed my eyes and shuddered as her arms folded round me and I felt a cold like nothing I had ever felt before. As if Ice was being poured into every bone. She was inside me. I could feel the cold of her in my lungs, my flesh, my heart. ' Thank you Tyler,' she was whispering and it was as if the voice was coming from somewhere deep inside me.

And then, the cold left me. I was free of her. She was gone from me. And at last I opened my eyes.

And knew real terror.

Because, when I opened my eyes I wasn't looking at Hayley Brown.

I was looking at me.

CHAPTER 22

It was as if I was looking into a mirror. Fair hair, held back by clasps, blue eyes, wearing my favourite red jacket and jeans. It was me and I was smiling.

I couldn't understand. ' What's happened....?'

I reached out towards the figure in front of me and I saw my hands. My legs went weak, because these were not my hands. I turned them round, studied them in horror. There were scars on my wrists, on my arms, the nails were broken and dirty and encrusted with blood. I looked at the dress I was wearing. It was a grey gown that once had been white, now it was discoloured and stained. I was wearing Hayley Brown's dress.

Why did it take me so long to figure out what had happened? I was too dazed to think straight, that was it. I just kept staring at me, at the me standing   at the other side of the room, not saying a word, my terror growing with every silent second.

' Thank you, Tyler.' This girl, this me, said. And it was my voice. Mine. ' I knew if you could come into my time, I sure as hell could get into yours. I knew if I got the chance I could become you.'

I shook my head. ' Can't happen. Can't be true.' And the voice I spoke with wasn't mine. It was Hayley Brown's. Now I screamed. ' No!'

' But it is true, Tyler,' she said, in my voice. ' We all know about you, we who wait on the other side. We all want you to help us. Only the strongest get through. And I'm strong, Tyler. I pushed my way ahead. But I didn't want you to help me. What good would that do me!' She sniggered. ' Stop me dying and then just leave me here? Locked in. Oh no. I wanted to be free. I wanted your life, Tyler. I wanted out of this place, and I found a way to do it.'

' You can't leave me here, I came here to help you.' But it was no use pleading with her. Her heart, my heart was stone.

Tyler Lawless bit her lip, in a gesture that was never mine. Trying to look cute? I never tried to look cute, did I? But *she* did. Hayley. She tossed my blonde head. ' I am going to have so much fun being you.'

She was backing toward the door, leaving me alone in this room. ' No,' it seemed to be all my terrified voice could say. 'No. Don't leave me.'

Tyler Lawless shrugged. ' Now you'll know what like it is to be locked up! '

I heard a bell ring shrilly, somewhere far away, in another time. She grinned. 'Have to go, that's visiting over. Jazz will be waiting for me.'

' Jazz'll know you're not me!' I shouted.

But she shook her head. ' How? Tell me?' Then she began to giggle hysterically. 'Honestly, don't you think this is definitely the most ingenious escape ever!'

I was going mad, that was what was going through my head. I was going mad. Or I was in some kind of a nightmare. I would wake up soon, because this couldn't be happening. She stood at the door for a moment, this version of myself. ' Have fun!' she said spitefully. Then she ran out of the door and left me.

I ran after her, but the second she was gone, the door was closed though I had not seen it shut. And I clawed at it. I banged against it. I screamed. I shouted. But she was gone. And then, only then, did I realise how sly she had been, Hayley Brown. How wicked she had been. This had been her plan all along. She hadn't wanted me to help her. She had wanted me to take her place. I had seen her desperation, but the desperation wasn't for me to help her, it was to escape. To get out of this place, start afresh, start a new life, as ME!

I slid to the floor. What did that make me? Her ghost? I looked at my arms, ragged with old scars, but solid. I even nipped the skin to see if I was still alive. And I winced when it hurt. What was I? Who was I? I banged again at the door and shouted . I didn't even know what time I was in, then, or now? I screamed as I had never screamed. ' Let me Out! Let! Me! Out!'

PART TWO

CHAPTER 23

Jazz was on her own when she saw Tyler come out of the house. Charlie had to go back, she said. She'd had a headache, she said. She kept asking for Tyler. Jazz knew she felt as if she was being deserted. ' Have I offended her?' Charlie had asked.

'Of course not, Charlie. I just don't think she feels well.' Jazz had told her. She was still worried about Charlie, but was dying to know what had happened to Tyler in that house. Had she seen Hayley Brown again? Had she helped her? Was it over at last?

Wow! She thought when she saw Tyler bounce down the steps. She looks so happy.

Jazz ran towards her. ' What happened?' She nodded to the house. ' You saw her again, didn't you?' she grabbed her arm. ' You look so happy. Have you sorted everything out? You did, didn't you?'

She'd found out whatever it was that Hayley wanted, she had made it right for her. Tyler stopped right in front of her and she began to laugh. Even Jazz had to laugh too when she heard her. It cheered her up. ' Come on, I'm all ears.'

For a second it was as if Tyler didn't recognise her. She looked at her, and then after a moment, she blinked. She was in one of her dreams, Jazz thought fondly. ' You saw her, didn't you?' She asked again.

Tyler linked her arm in Jazz's. ' Oh yes, I saw her, everything's going to be great now.'

' But what did she want?'

' She wanted me to pass on to Doctor Crow that she's happy now. She forgives her.'

Jazz stopped. She couldn't help but feel disappointed. It wasn't exactly the dramatic climax she hoped for. ' She forgives her? So...Doctor Crow killed her, but she forgives her...just like that.'

' Oh yes, but she's at peace. She wants me...us to forget about her.'

Jazz was puzzled. ' But if she told you Dr Crow killed her, shouldn't we try to bring her to justice? I mean, she came back to tell you that she wants you to forget about her? That's it? We didn't even know she existed before she came to you.'

Tyler looked a bit annoyed, and that wasn't like her at all. ' She wanted me to tell this doctor she forgives her. Okay. She really is a thoughtful girl, Hayley Brown. Doctor Crow got her a lot of bad press she didn't deserve.' She pulled Jazz on. ' Let's get out of this place, It gives me the creeps.'

' Aren't you going to ask about Charlie?'

' Who's he?'

Jazz pulled herself free. But she was laughing. ' Who's *he*? *He* is a girl, what is wrong with you, Tyler?'

' I've just spoken to a ghost. I'm allowed to be a bit mixed up, right.'

Of course that was true, but she said it in such a snappy way it surprised Jazz. ' I told Charlie we would see her next week, maybe take her out.'

' We don't have to come back here anymore.' Tyler said. ' I'm finished with Hayley Brown. I'm finished with this place.'

Jazz was puzzled. ' But we're coming back for Charlie.'

But Tyler wasn't listening. She was running ahead of Jazz. She'd seen the bus. 'Come on, hurry. We're going to miss it.'

CHAPTER 24

How long had I been locked in this room? I felt as if I'd been here forever. Screaming and shouting ever since Hayley Brown had walked out of the door, as me. No one had answered me. No one had come near me.

How could I have been so stupid? That's what she'd been waiting for, that's why she had been so desperate for me to come here. To take me over. That's all she had ever wanted. There was an evil in Hayley Brown. Jazz had warned me, everyone had warned me, and I had been too stupid to see it.

But how had she done it? How did she know how to do it? To come to me, wrap her arms around me, get inside of me, pass through me, become me?

Was her plan to leave me here forever? Of course it was, she'd never come back here to Bonaventure House. To be locked in here. I was going to be stuck in her body forever. Locked in. Trapped. And she would be in mine. Free. Taking over my life. My friends.

I slumped down on the floor, exhausted and frightened. Surely someone would see the difference, my mother would surely know, or my dad. Jazz, Mac, my other friends?

But even if they saw differences, they would never think it wasn't me inside her. How could anyone believe such an unbelievable thing? That Hayley Brown had walked through me and taken over my body?

I began to rock back and forth on the floor, hugging my knees. She was me. I was her.

I started screaming again. Couldn't stop myself, crawled to the door and clawed at it with my nails till they were raw and bleeding.

At last someone came. I heard the footsteps come closer and I got to my feet. Someone was opening the door. I was silent. I stepped back.

One of the Sisters, a young woman, opened the door. She looked stern. ' What is all this commotion, Hayley?'

I sobbed my story out. ' You have to listen to me. I am not Hayley Brown.'

She raised her eyes. ' Oh Hayley, for goodness sake.'

' No-honestly- you have to believe me.' I swallowed hard, tried to speak slowly and as sensibly as I could. 'Something happened and she left. Hayley Brown left, in my body, and she left me trapped in here.'

'Hayley, we don't want to lock you in, we want you to join the other girls, but you have to stop all this.'

'Please don't lock me in. You have to help me. My name is Tyler Lawless. I'm not Hayley Brown. I'm not!'

She began shaking her head, and turned to leave me and I couldn't stay calm. Could you? I clutched at her arm, and I began to yell again. ' My name is Tyler Lawless!'

She pulled away as if she was afraid of me. ' I f you keep this up, Hayley I'll have to call Doctor Crow.'

Doctor Crow. Doctor Crow. I could explain it all to her. ' Yes. Yes, call Doctor Crow. She'll understand.'

It was a faint hope, that someone with a link to the future could help me here in the past.

But it was the best hope I had. I grabbed for her again. ' Yes. Get Doctor Crow.'

****

'So, where are we going tonight?' Tyler asked as they sat on the bus.

Jazz had never seen her so happy. ' Tonight? Nowhere.'

' It's Saturday night, come on. We have to go out somewhere. Celebrate.'

' We're skint, zero money. Have you forgotten? '

Tyler let out a big sigh. ' Can't we borrow it from somewhere? I'll ask her mum.'

' You'll ask....whose mum? Tyler, what is wrong with you?'

Tyler had an expression on her face Jazz had never seen before. She looked as if she was on the verge of a temper. She tutted in annoyance. ' I meant my mum.'

'Are you sure you're all right?' Jazz asked.

 Then Tyler's face broke into a smile and she was more like the old Tyler again. 'Just so relieved it's all over with Hayley Brown. Glad to see the back of her. That's why I want us to celebrate.'

' You're the only one I know who had a good word to say about her.'

' Maybe I knew her better than anyone else.' Then Tyler giggled as if she knew something Jazz didn't.

' What's the joke?'

Tyler shook her head. ' Nothing.'

Jazz sighed. ' Anyway, you never have a bad word to say about anyone.'

Tyler tutted. ' You make me sound so boring.'

' You're not boring. Come on,' Jazz whispered. ' A girl who can see the dead? Nothing boring about that.'

CHAPTER 25

I don't even know how I managed to sleep, but I did, and I even dreamed. I dreamed this was all a nightmare and I was home. Hayley Brown had tried to take me over, and she had failed. I had escaped. My mum was making a Sunday roast chicken dinner. I could almost smell it. I was setting the table, putting blue plates I had never seen before on a long table. I was so happy, and there was an old song playing on the radio and I was singing along with it. ' All I have to do is dream....'

And then I was awake, and it wasn't a dream. I was here, locked in. The early light of day was coming through the window. I tried to open it, but it wouldn't budge. I ran for the door, and tugged and it was still locked. I slid to the floor. The nightmare was real.

I had no idea how long I sat there on the floor before there was a knock on the door. 'Breakfast, Hayley,' the voice was cheery. Not the voice of the nun who had come last night.

I scrambled to my feet.

' Move back from the door, Hayley,' the friendly voice asked. I stepped back. The door opened. A nun was there carrying a tray. She wasn't alone. Another woman was with her and she didn't look like a nun at all. In fact if it hadn't been for the lipstick and the hairstyle I would have taken her for a man. She looked more like a bodyguard. Was Hayley Brown so dangerous they weren't allowed to be with her on their own?

Of course she was. Now, I knew how dangerous she actually was.

' If you behave today, Hayley, you might get the chance to join the other girls for a while. But you will have to promise to behave.'

The nun put the tray down on the table by the window. I wanted to swipe everything to the floor, see the cup and the plate smash into pieces, and the toast and the cereal fly onto the floor. I could imagine Hayley

Brown doing that every day. Was I becoming like her already? Is that what would happen to me if I stayed in this place for too long?

' Do you need the toilet?' the Sister asked.

I nodded. I would have agreed to anything to get out of this room.

They both came with me, the nun and the bodyguard. They led me down the corridor to the toilets. There were two cubicles, a couple of shower units and a row of sinks. I stepped into the end cubicle. There was a small window high on the wall. Small, but wide enough for me , even in Hayley Brown's body, to squeeze through. If the nun hadn't stayed in the toilets waiting for me, I would have tried to open it. I would have escaped. But there was no chance of that, not now.

' I'd rather eat with the other girls,' I said as we headed back to room 4. I didn't want to go in there again. ' I promise I'll behave.'

The young nun touched my arm. ' Maybe at lunchtime, Hayley. Depending on what Doctor Crow says.'

I couldn't hide my excitement. ' Doctor Crow. She's coming? This morning?' I wanted so much to see her. I would explain everything. She knew how bad Hayley Brown was. ' Born bad,' hadn't she told me that herself.

Capable of doing something as bad as this, I would tell her, and she would believe me.

I was so glad to hear she was coming that I didn't contradict the nun again when she called me Hayley. I let them lock me in again, and I even sat and ate the breakfast they'd left for me.

CHAPTER 26

Jazz watched Tyler sprawl along the bench in the dining hall. ' Anybody fancy bunking off this afternoon.'

Aisha almost fell off her seat. ' You're suggesting bunking off? You, Tyler- I never break the rules-Lawless?'

' Maybe for a change I want to live up to my name. Law-less.' And she laughed.

' It's English next. We don't want to miss that,' Jazz said.

Tyler screwed up her face.

' It's your favourite subject,' Jazz reminded her, though the thought went through her head, why should she need to be reminded?

' People change,' Tyler said. She twirled a lock of her hair through her fingers and smiled at Callum. 'You want to bunk off with me, Callum.'

Callum's face went bright red. ' Me?' Aisha slid closer to him on the bench.

Was Tyler actually flirting with Callum? That seemed impossible to believe.

Tyler suddenly sat up. Let out a long bored sigh. Jazz had never seen her friend look bored. ' Are you feeling okay, Tyler?'

Tyler held her gaze for a moment, then she looked away. Did she look embarrassed? No, Jazz, thought, she looked more nervous than embarrassed. She stood up from the table and began to walk fast out of the dining hall. Jazz hurried after her. ' Is everything alright, Tyler?'

' Course it is. I'm fine. Don't I look fine?' she brushed her hair back with her hand. ' Is something wrong with me?'

' It's just that, you haven't been the same since we were at Bonaventure House. Did something happen there? Something to do with Hayley Brown?'

She stopped. She swung back. ' Yes, that' s it.' She beamed a big smile. ' Something happened that really scared me, made me realise you have to make the most of every moment. I can't talk about it now, I will tell you one day, Jazz. 'She touched Jazz's arm. ' So if I say something wrong, or do anything, you will understand, won't you?'

And then, before Jazz could answer her, she turned and ran ahead of her.

Tyler was behaving strangely, but something must have happened on Saturday. And when she was ready to tell Jazz about it, she would. Jazz would just have to be patient.

CHAPTER 27

Dr. Crow didn't come on the Sunday. I was out of the room only for Mass, and sat through the whole service flanked by the bodyguard again, and another nun. Then I was taken back in once more and the door was locked. Every time I heard footsteps on the corridor outside, I would call out and ask when the doctor coming, had she phoned? I didn't give up hope she would come even when the lights went out and the room was plunged into a darkness that terrified me. I didn't sleep much, lying awake, hoping she would come in the night.

It was next morning before she came. Along with breakfast. Here she was as I had seen her when she had struggled with Hayley Brown. There were no grey streaks in her so black hair, It was sleek and held back from her face in a clasp. Her eyes were bright, and she had cheekbones like blades. Her face looked more than a little annoyed when the door opened and she stepped inside. When I leapt toward her she didn't flinch.

' You have to get me out of here, Doctor Crow. I don't belong here.' I tried to grab at her hand. She pushed it away. ' I'm not Hayley Brown. I am not her!'

How stupid it sounded, even to me. She didn't look surprised, or even puzzled with the story I was telling for she hardly reacted. She only sighed. ' Well, this is a new one.'

' It's not a lie. It's the truth. I know, I know, it sounds unbelievable, but it is true.' I had to make her believe me, help me. She knew how bad Hayley Brown was, bad to the bone, she'd said. She would understand what she was capable of.

' Please, just listen. Hayley Brown took over my body. Became me. I don't know how. I wanted to help her, but all the time all she wanted was to become me. You said yourself she was born bad.' I knew as I watched her expression I had lost her.

' You should be a writer, Hayley, where do you come up with these things?'

' I'm not making it up. It's the truth. I am not Hayley Brown.'

' I'm a psychiatrist, Hayley. I really want to help you, but all you do is lie and cause trouble, and attack people.'

I tried again. Desperate. ' I know where you live.'

A reaction at last. ' Is that a threat?'

' No. No. I'm trying to let you know I'm telling the truth. I don't belong here. I've been to your house, I've met your mother. She gave us tea, but there was nothing in the pot.' I remembered too late that was in the future. It hadn't happened for her yet. It sounded even crazier now.

She stepped back, I could see the alarm in her face. ' When were out at my house?' Before I could answer her she called out.' Sister!'

I'd said it all wrong, but how do you explain something like this. I tried again. 'Not in this time....in the future. I live in the future. Please, listen.'

But she wasn't listening to me anymore. Sister came in the door. ' Has she been allowed out at any time?' she asked the nun.

' Of course not.' She sounded offended it had even been suggested.

I tried to protest. ' No, no. You don't understand....'

No one listened. It was as if I wasn't there at all.

' She's lying,' Sister said. ' trying to frighten you. You know she's done that before.' She said it in a whisper, but I could make out every word.

I grabbed at Doctor Crow's coat. ' I am not Hayley Brown. My name is Tyler. Tyler Lawless.'

The Sister said. ' That's what she's calling herself today. Tyler Lawless.'

' I *am* Tyler Lawless. ' I grabbed at her. ' You have to help me. You're my only hope.'

But the doctor shook herself free of me. Without another word she stepped out of the room. The door closed. I was alone, and trapped once again.

CHAPTER 28

' What have you done to your hair, Tyler?' Jazz was waiting for her at the school gates. She hardly recognised the Tyler who stepped off the bus. Her hair was lighter, blonder, swept up and held in a gold clasp. She looked older. Jazz saw some of the boys glance her way.

Tyler flicked her fingers at it. ' Like it? I've always wanted to wear my hair this way,' she said as she came close.

' Have you dyed it? It makes you look so....different,' Jazz said.

Tyler laughed so loudly people turned to look at her. A phoney laugh, meant to be noticed. 'Maybe it's time for a change,' she said.

'You don't need to change. I kind of like you the way you are,' it was Mac, coming up behind them.

And Tyler turned and tapped him under the chin. 'Course you do,' she said.

Usually if Mac said something complimentary, Tyler blushed. Blushed to the roots. Now, it was Mac who blushed. Not used to Tyler flirting with him.

'Do you like my hair like this, honey?' She smiled up at him, and, did she flutter her eyelashes! And....honey? She had called Mac 'honey'?

Jazz grabbed her arm and pulled her away. 'Come on, you're beginning to embarrass me.'

Tyler laughed again as she walked with Jazz up the long drive to the school entrance, glancing over her shoulder at Mac, making sure he was still watching. And he was, but he looked puzzled.

'What's got into you, Tyler?'

'I think you're jealous, Jazz.' She said with a giggle. 'I've got great hair, have you ever noticed? Thick as anything, and a great colour. Tyler Lawless never appreciated it or made the most of it.'

Jazz stopped dead. ' What do you mean, Tyler Lawless never appreciated it?'

For a moment, Tyler did look a bit embarrassed. ' I only meant...the old Tyler Lawless. This is me...' she flicked at her hair again. ' the new Tyler Lawless. This is the first day of the rest of my life.'

She strode on ahead of Jazz and she seemed to revel in the way the other pupils were watching her. Especially the boys. Why was she acting like that? What had gotten into her?

If this was the new Tyler Lawless, Jazz wasn't sure that she liked her.

CHAPTER 29

I cried myself to sleep. Hardly got up out of the bed all that day. Nothing I had said had helped. In fact, I had only made things worse. Doctor Crow thought I had been threatening her- I knew where she lived- and how could I blame her? Hayley Brown had threatened her before this. Hayley Brown had attacked her.

A terrible thought came to me. I was never going to get away from here. There was no way I could convince anyone I was not Hayley Brown. Hayley Brown died soon, days from now, in this locked room, died by her own hand. Or *was* it by her own hand? She had told me Doctor Crow had murdered her. But could I believe anything Hayley Brown had said after this? Yet, the knife...how had the knife got in here with her. Did Doctor

Crow have a secret part in her death? Was I going to become so desperate, so terrified that I would kill myself?

No. No. No. Don't let that happen. I won't let that happen.

I lay on my back and looked up at the window. I could see clouds scurry past the moon, branches of a tree brushed against the glass. Would I ever be able to touch that tree, any tree again? Would I ever run through the grass? The thought made me sob into my pillow. I had never missed my mum so much as I did in that moment, or my dad. How I wished I could call Jazz. Had she noticed any difference? Jazz had a psychic side- I knew that- was something telling her that this Tyler wasn't the real one? I prayed that there was.

But even if she suspected, how could she possibly imagine the truth? It was all too unbelievable.

Hopeless.

It was all hopeless. I would never get away from here. I would die here, on November 27th. Only a few days from now.

Unless.

I shot up in bed. Unless...I changed the past. Unless, I got out of this place. If I wasn't here, I couldn't die in a locked room. In that moment I knew I had only one hope.

I was going to escape.

****

Jazz's phone was ringing. She looked at the number. It was Tyler's but not her mobile. She was ringing from home.

Tyler had been strange today, Jazz thought, bored in lessons, even in English, usually her favourite subject. Jazz had watched her filing her nails under her desk.

Filing her nails. Tyler? The only girl Jazz knew who had no hint of vanity about her.

No interest in her hair, in her nails. All of a sudden, she was vain.

Even the boys had noticed. ' I told her she was looking good, and do you know what she said?' Adam had told her that afternoon. ' " Eat your heart out Adam." And she blew me a kiss! Tyler, and she didn't even blush.'

And they had all asked the same question, Mac and Callum and Aisha too. 'What's got into Tyler?'

Jazz picked up the phone. ' Hi Tyler,' she said.

But it wasn't Tyler. It was her mum.

' Jazz, I'm a bit worried about Tyler.'

Jazz sat down before she asked. ' Worried about her? Why?'

It seemed hard for Mrs. Lawless to go on. ' She's so snappy, with all of us, even Steven. And Tyler's never bad tempered. Her and Steven always have a laugh together.'

' She has been a bit different at school,' Jazz said feebly. She didn't want to betray her friend completely.

' She dyed her hair, did you see that?' Mrs. Lawless didn't wait for an answer. 'Then she shouted at me when I said she was too young for that. ' She took a deep breath. ' Was she out with you on Saturday night, Jazz?'

' Me? No?' It was out before Jazz could stop herself.

' She told us she was. She went out, all dressed up, and she came in late and said she was with you, and I didn't believe her. She never tells lies, Jazz. Why is she doing it now? Is she worried about something?'

The thought of Hayley Brown crossed Jazz's mind, but how could she tell Mrs. Lawless about that? Tyler had sworn her to secrecy, and anyway, that was over, surely. But she would definitely ask her about it tomorrow.

' She's not got a boyfriend has she?' Mrs. Lawless knew about Mac, but theirs was such an innocent friendship, hardly a romance.

' Tyler still likes Mac, and he likes her.'

' I know, and it's lovely that you all go out together. But I thought she might have met someone she doesn't want me to know about.'

Jazz answered her at once. ' No. Definitely not.'

She could hear Mrs. Lawless's sigh of relief. ' It's just all this dying her hair, painting her nails...it's just not Tyler, is it?'

And Jazz agreed. ' No, it's just not Tyler.'

' Will you let me know if you do find out anything Jazz? I know you won't want to betray a secret, but I'm just so worried. '

' Leave it with me,' Jazz said.

Mrs. Lawless sounded relieved. ' You're a good friend, Jazz.'

CHAPTER 30

I had to wait till it was dark before I could attempt to make my escape. But I prepared for it throughout the day. Every time I went to the toilet,(and why weren't they suspicious at how often I had to go to the toilet that day?) I would use the end cubicle, with the window hidden from view, and each time I would open the window, and close it again making sure it was loose enough for me to open later. It was only a tiny window. Would I fit through? Me, Tyler Lawless would. But Hayley Brown? I dismissed that fear. I would fit through. I would make sure of it, I would imagine my body like rubber, like elastic, because I had to get out of here and this was my only chance.

Escaping was all I thought about all day. I went over again and again, how I was going to do it. I would be taken again to the toilet before bedtime, taken there after the other girls had finished, and for once it would suit me to be alone.   I saw myself sliding through that window easily, and then....and then what? My stomach was doing somersaults. I'd never done anything like this before. Never thought I would ever have to consider escaping from prison. I didn't know the layout of this place.   Where I was going to go?   I was in a different time. Fifteen years ago the town would look different. Buildings that had been torn down would still be there, estates built in my time would be something else now. My mum, my dad, where had they lived fifteen years ago? Before I was born? Fifteen years ago, Steven would just have been a baby. I couldn't remember where they had lived.   Jazz wouldn't be born either.   I didn't know who I was going to go to, or where I was going to go. I just knew I had to get out of here.

My mind panicked. It was all going to go wrong.

And then I remembered my gran. My gran would be alive, and I knew where my gran had lived.   In my mind I pictured the flat in town, with the high roofs and the big front room and the cupboards where I had hidden when I was little.   She would be there, still alive, and somehow I knew that she would understand and believe me.   My gran had known things, I

167

realised that now. Part of my gift had come from her. She was my guardian angel, and she would help me. That's where I would head.

Before lights out, one of the young nuns, Sister Angelus, came to take me to the toilet. I was relieved to see the manly bodyguard wasn't with her. The house, silent and still, was locked up for the night. I prayed she wouldn't stay with me. She didn't. She stood for a moment inside the toilets, then with a nod and a smile she said.

' I'll come back in ten minutes, Hayley. Give you some privacy. Okay.'

She thought there was no where I could go, no escape.

The second she was gone I was inside the end cubicle and had locked the door. Then, I clambered up onto the cistern so I could reach the window, and after a couple of tugs it squeaked open and I pushed it wide.

Too loud! I held my breath, waiting for footsteps clattering down the corridor, waiting for the door to be pushed open. But after a moment, I knew no one had heard. I pushed at the window again and with one backward look, and a prayer, I squeezed through.

It was freezing cold outside, the temperature had suddenly dropped after a day of rain, and all I was wearing was a flimsy night dress, a cotton dressing gown and slippers. I jumped to the ground and my feet sank into the still soft earth. It didn't take long for the damp to seep through to my feet, for the cold to burn into my bones. But it was more nerves than cold that made my teeth chatter. The cold couldn't hurt me, I told myself, not yet. I could bear it. All the time I was thinking about how I would get to my gran's house. As I ran I went over in my head the route I would take. Once out of the grounds, I would head for the main road, keeping close to the trees that bordered each side of the street. The main road eventually led to the motorway, and then I could follow that and it would lead me to town. I would have to walk for miles, but I would be free, and heading for my gran.

I stopped behind a tree and from here I could see the main gates. Now there was no candy striped bar, no security gate I could easily slip through. Not now, in this time. Instead, there was a high iron gate with chains wound round the railings and secured with a heavy padlock. Could I climb over? I decided against that. There were floodlights there and it would be too easy to spot me. Anyway, I wasn't good at climbing. My eyes followed the stone wall that ran all along the perimeter of the estate disappearing into darkness. That hadn't changed. Still the same as it was in my time. There was barbed wire at the top but at least there would be no modern security systems installed either. No CCTV. Not then. I could risk the barbed wire.

I felt my way along the wall in the dark, looking for a place where I could climb and leap over. I had to move fast. All the time I listened for an alarm being raised, for people to come shouting, running after me.

I was so intent on listening that I didn't watch where I was going, and my foot caught on a boulder and down I went. Fell flat on my face, my cheek slapped against the stone. I bit my lip to keep from yelling with the pain. I dragged myself up and then I realised that maybe that boulder could be a godsend. It was big enough for me to stand on. If I could lift it and carry it to the wall, I could use it as a stepping stone to reach the top. Where did I get the strength? I don't know. Desperation, I suppose. I couldn't bear the thought of going back into that room. This was my last chance, my only chance. I struggled with the boulder and dropped it at the bottom of the wall, and stood on it.

The first time I threw myself up I almost gripped the top, but my fingers caught on the barbed wire and it ripped at my skin. I slipped to the ground again. Don't cry out, Tyler, I told myself. I took a deep breath and tried once more. This time I was ready for the pain. This time, I kept hold though the wire bit deep into my hand. I dragged myself up. My feet scrabbled on the stone. The pain in my hands was excruciating. One of my slippers came off, tumbling to the ground. When they found it they would know where I had climbed over. Didn't matter. I hoped to be long gone by that time. Finally I was straddling the wall. And the wire was biting into my legs. I wiped my hands on the dressing gown and drew long smears of blood on it. There were scraps of material stuck on the wire. Were they a sign that other girls had attempted to escape this way, just like me?

My hands were bleeding , but I would bear the pain, I could bear any pain. I was going to make it.

CHAPTER 31

Tyler stepped off the school bus and Jazz had to look twice at her, sure she was not seeing the real Tyler. She shouted. ' Are you wearing makeup?'

Tyler's hair was swept back, and pinned up on top of her head. She was wearing some kind of foundation, and her eyes were a lot darker than nature intended them to be. She said it again. ' Are you wearing make up?'

Tyler brushed past her. ' So?'

' Tyler, you know we're not allowed to wear make up in school. It's against the rules.'

Tyler turned round to her and laughed. ' Time to change the rules then.'

Jazz pulled her back. ' What's got into you, Tyler?'

She pulled herself free. ' O come on, Jazz, lighten up.'

' What's next? Tattoes? Nose rings?'

' Mm..there's a thought,' replied Tyler.

' This is all since Saturday, Tyler,' Jazz said. ' Something happened with that Hayley Brown, it changed you. Now tell me what it was!'

Tyler looked alarmed when she said that. Then she shouted back at her. ' Forget about blinking Hayley Brown. I never want to hear her name again.' She stomped away from her up the drive towards the school entrance.

They had hardly spoken the rest of the day. It hurt Jazz. She saw Tyler hanging round with some older girls that they would never talk to before, troublemakers all of them. She even ignored Mac, and when had Tyler ever done that ? She'd have to get to the bottom of this, Jazz thought, whatever had changed her, it was all linked with Hayley Brown.

She caught up with Tyler at the end of the day as they both headed down the long drive to the school gates. ' Don't want to fight,' she said.

' Neither do I,' Tyler smiled, but there was no apology in her voice.

' It's just....you don't seem to be yourself.'

Suddenly, Tyler swung round. ' What do you mean by that! What a silly thing to say. Who else do you think I am!' She looked guilty for some reason, Jazz was sure of it.

Jazz was taken aback. ' Didn't mean anything. Just a figure of speech.' Why had it made Tyler so angry? It was spiralling into another quarrel and Jazz didn't want that.

It seemed neither did Tyler. ' Oh, I know you didn't Jazz, let's just forget it, eh?' But again, there was no real apology in her tone. She just wanted to stop talking about it.

Jazz was just about to say, why don't you come to my house tonight, but the words never had time to come. There was a whisper from somewhere nearby. ' Jazz. Tyler.'

They both turned. ' Who's that?'

The voice had come from the bushes. . At first they could see nothing. Jazz stepped closer. A face suddenly appeared, a frightened face streaked with tears.

' I've run away. Are you going to help me?'

It was Charlie.

CHAPTER 31

The drop on the other side of the wall was death defying, at least to me. The ground seemed to be miles away. I sat at the top, rocking back and forth, trying to give myself the courage to leap. I was sweating blood, even though I was freezing cold. I so wished I didn't have to do this. My other slipper had been pulled from my foot as I'd swung my leg over the wall. Now my feet were bare and ice cold and wet. My flimsy nightdress caught on the barbed wire and I tried to pull it free, but a scrap remained joining the others there. I wanted to put off the moment when I would have to jump. It looked so far, and there wasn't even a proper pavement, just jagged stones and grass. I was sure I would break something when I landed, or worse.

So, what do you want Tyler. To stay here, or go?

I glanced behind me. From here I could see the house. A light flicked on in one of the windows . Quickly followed by another. I imagined Sister Angelus running from the toilets, going from room to room, knocking doors, alerting everyone. They'd noticed I was missing. No time to hesitate. I leapt.

Pain seared up my leg as soon as I hit the ground. One foot scraped on stone, the other sank into soil that was just beginning to freeze. I tumbled back and smacked my head against the hard ground. For a moment I thought I was going to lose consciousness. I pushed my fist into my mouth to stop myself from screaming out in pain. Couldn't stop now. Couldn't waste time. Within seconds, in spite of the pain, I was on my feet. I began to hobble, heading down the hill, keeping close to the wall. If I could make it to the main road, I would keep to the woods, hiding there, I would follow the road, head home, head to my gran's house. She would know what to do. That was the only thing that kept me going. My gran would know what to do.

If I could just make it to the main road.

All the way I kept looking back, watching for the headlights of a car turn out of the gates, coming closer, searching me out. Listened for alarms sounding.

And all the time I kept thinking that only two days ago, I was at school, laughing with my friends, and now, I was an escaped prisoner, on the run, in another time. Me, Tyler Lawless.

I glanced back to see a car was heading down the road towards me, the headlights coming closer. I pressed myself into the bushes, crouched down on the ground, making myself as invisible as I could.

The car whizzed past. An old Morris Minor. Not from Bonaventure House at all. I realised I hadn't been breathing. I was shaking with fear, with cold, my teeth chattering. I came out of the bushes and looked up the dark road. I began to run again.

****

' Charlie, what have you done?' Jazz pulled her back into the bushes out of sight of anyone who might be watching. Tyler came behind her. Charlie clutched at Jazz's hand. ' You are going to help me, aren't you?'

' What do you expect us to do?' It was Tyler who asked and her voice was so harsh Jazz swung round.

' What are you talking like that for? Can't you see she's scared?' she turned back to Charlie. ' Did something else happen, Charlie?'

' Who did you steal from this time?' Tyler almost snapped at her.

' I didn't steal it, I tried to tell her that. I found it. I tried to explain....'

' Oh here we go again.' Tyler pushed forward. ' You never steal do you?'

Charlie tugged at Jazz's jacket. 'Please don't make me go back. She says she's going to kill me this time....and if I have to go back, I'll kill myself. I will.'

' Don't be so melodramatic. We could get into a lot of trouble helping you,' Tyler said. ' You should go back and face up to what you've done.'

' I'm sorry, I'm really sorry,' Charlie said.

Jazz hadn't said a word. She was too stunned by the way Tyler was talking. It was Charlie she spoke to. ' Of course we're going to help you, Charlie.' She shot Tyler a dark look. ' We're going to help you and hide you till we figure out what to do. Okay.'

CHAPTER 32

The road from Bonaventure House led down under the old railway bridge and then onto the motorway. Once I was there I could at least hide for a while. Rest. There was a path that swung round behind the bridge and led to an old ramblers' footpath, running parallel to the motorway. Lonely and quiet, I could follow that road towards town. But that bridge never seemed to be getting any closer. I knew I must look like some kind of wild woman, my hair was standing on end, my dress torn and bloody. I was barefoot. My face was bruised and scratched. My hands were bleeding. Terrible thought, in a mind filled with terrible thoughts, in just a few days time Hayley brown would die, her face bruised and bloody, just as mine was now. If I went back there I would be dying her death, just as she did. I couldn't go back there. I couldn't. I would die there. Die in her place.

And what if I couldn't convince my gran? I knew she would help me, if I could convince her that this was me...Tyler, who hadn't even been born yet! My deepest fear was that gran *wouldn't* believe me. It was too much to hope for. But I couldn't give up.

I was so caught up in these terrifying thoughts, that I hardly heard the purring of the car coming behind me. It was the headlights I saw first. I glanced behind me. It was travelling slowly, and though I could not make out the people inside, I could see the beam from torches searching out each side of the road. Searching for me. No, not me. They were searching for Hayley Brown. I could not lose my identity. I would remain Tyler Lawless.

I tried to run again, and I tripped over stones and grass. I dragged myself to my feet, and thrust myself between some bushes at the edge of the road. The bushes weren't thick enough to camouflage me, but there were thicker trees up ahead, if I could make it there, I could hide. But my leg ached. I felt it was ready to crumple under me. I winced with every step I took.

The car was coming closer. I stopped dead, pressed myself as far into the bushes as I could. The car headlights moved past me, and I almost breathed a sigh of relief. I took the chance to move towards the thicker trees. And at that moment the torchlight swung back and found me. I felt like a rabbit caught in the middle of the road. I couldn't move. I just stared.

The beam of light enveloped me. It trapped me. I turned away at last, threw my arms across my eyes, as if, like when I was a little girl, if I couldn't see them, they couldn't possibly see me. Then, I started running again, running and screaming.

Stupid! I wasn't made for escaping, not me, not Tyler Lawless. What did I know of escaping! I should have headed the other way. Or climbed up onto the railway track, leapt on a train. I should have gone anywhere else but here, and then they would not have caught me.

Or would they? Was this really my destiny? I kept running. Heard footsteps behind me, too close, then a voice.

' Hayley! No one's going to hurt you. Come back!'

I was trying not to cry. I screamed out. 'I am not Hayley Brown!' And all I could think of still was that if I could just make it to the motorway, I'd be safe. I'd be free.

I felt a hand on my shoulder.

And I was still screaming.

****

Jazz took Charlie home with her. Tyler refused. Though it would have been easier for Tyler to take Charlie. Tyler's house had a garage, Charlie could easily have slept in there, in the car, just for tonight. Yet, Tyler, that compassionate soft hearted friend of hers, had suddenly turned to stone. 'I'm not getting involved,' she'd said.

Charlie couldn't understand it either. 'I'm so sorry I annoyed Tyler. I didn't mean to.'

'I don't know what's come over her, Charlie.'

Charlie had an answer. 'It's because she thinks I stole her phone, isn't it?'

But Jazz knew that wasn't the reason.

When she got home, Jazz told her mum that Charlie was a new classmate who needed a bit of help with homework. Her mum didn't even raise an eyebrow. Jazz was always bringing home strays, her mum knew that. But Jazz help anyone with homework? If she did, that would be a first.

She knew too that Charlie couldn't stay for the night. ' My mum's daft as a brush, Charlie, but even she would want to contact your family. So your mum and dad wouldn't worry about you. Or she'd want to drive you home herself.'

' It's okay, Jazz, I don't have to stay the night. Just give me something to eat, give me a loan of one of your old jackets. Maybe if you can spare a few pounds. I'll go on the run. People do it all the time and they never get found.'

Jazz felt like crying. Charlie meant it. She would do it if she had to. 'I'll kill myself if I go back,' she had said, over and over, as if she meant it.

' I don't want you to go on the run, Charlie.'

' I'm not going back, Jazz. I'm never going back there.'

Mum let her eat her dinner in her room, along with Charlie, and Jazz watched as Charlie wolfed down the macaroni cheese as if it was the best thing she'd ever tasted. And later she stuffed an old rucksack with some spare clothes, sandwiches and apples and a bottle of water. She put in socks and she looked out one of last year's jackets. And Charlie was so grateful, Jazz wanted to cry for her. ' This is brilliant, Jazz. How can I ever thank you?'

' I don't even know if I'm doing the right thing.'

' I'll be fine. I'll get a train to Glasgow. I've got some money. I'll send you a postcard from London.' She said it as if this was the beginning of a great adventure.

'They'll be looking for you, Charlie.' Jazz reminded her.

' Oh, I'm not exactly on Britain's most wanted list.' She was quiet for a moment. Then she laughed, and it was the saddest sound Jazz had ever heard. ' In fact, nobody wants me.'

' But your family,' Jazz said. ' You've got a nice family.'

Charlie shook her head. ' 'Yeah, I know, but I've let them down so often. I can't go to them. They deserve better than me. I'll go off and make my fortune and then I'll come back rich and they'll love me. Someone's got to love me sometime, haven't they?'

And that only made Jazz feel even more like crying. Charlie thought she had to be rich to be loved.

Charlie went on in a cheery voice. ' Do you know when I can get a train?'

There was a small unmanned station close to where Jazz lived. ' There's trains every twenty minutes to the city. I'll walk you there,' she said, though she wished she could think of something else to do. Somewhere to hide her till tomorrow. Jazz needed someone to talk to, someone to help her....and Tyler hadn't even called.

CHAPTER 33

They had to drag me back screaming to Bonaventure House. I was bundled into the car and nothing they said would console me. I wasn't in trouble, they assured me. The sisters wanted me to have a bath or a shower, change my clothes, but I refused, struggling against them. And in those moments I was no longer Tyler Lawless. I was turning into vicious, uncontrollable Hayley Brown. Finally, they gave in, and I was left, bruised and dirty in that room again. When the door locked behind me I threw myself on the bed and my screams turned to sobs. Now, I'd never convince anyone I was not Hayley Brown.

And Hayley Brown was going to die in just a few days.

Yet, I managed to fall asleep. Dreaming of Jazz, dreaming of her coming to rescue me. Dreaming of opening my eyes in the morning, and not being here.

I jumped awake when I heard the door being unlocked. It was Sister Angela. 'Hayley, Dr. Crow has come to see you.'

Was it still night, early morning? I didn't know. I leapt to my feet. Dr. Crow walked in. She sat in the chair by the window and stared at me for a time. ' Where did you plan to go, Hayley?'

I wiped the tears from my eyes, must have been crying in my sleep. ' My name is Tyler Lawless,' I said. I would never give up my identity.

' Oh please, Hayley. Not this again.'

I stepped toward her. I wanted to grab her by the shoulders and make her listen. ' It's the only way I can explain why I ran away, and where I planned to go. Please listen. Why can't you understand? Why would I say I was Tyler Lawless if I wasn't? I am Tyler Lawless. I am!'

She put her hands together so her fingertips were touching. ' I don't believe you because you always have some new ruse to excuse your bad behaviour. Remember the time you tried to say you had a split personality ? Or you'd been hypnotised by the Government to do bad things. I thought I had heard them all, but this is definitely a new one. Now you don't just have a split personality. You're a different person.'

' This isn't a lie!' I yelled at her. ' But I'm beginning to understand why Hayley Brown was so horrible. No wonder she tries to get out of here. No wonder she's wild and crazy. She's treated like an animal in here. And look at the background she's had, no family that cares about her. Maybe I would have turned out like her with a background like that.'

Dr. Crow's brow furrowed in a puzzled frown. ' What's this? Making up a new past for yourself? You have a decent family, Hayley Brown. They've forgiven you for so much. You don't deserve them. They care about you...too much in my opinion. They've never given up on you. So don't blame your family for the way you've turned out. You were born bad.'

Now I was puzzled. ' What do you mean? A decent family?'

I tried to search in my memory, Hayley had been born here, had almost been adopted, but the couple had been killed in a freak accident, and so she was left, to rot here, taken, when they could be bothered, by her useless family.

Who had told me that?

Charlie.

Charlie, who always told lies. All I believed about Hayley's life, was a lie!

'I'll have to let them know about this, of course,' Doctor Crow said.

'Don't tell them!' I yelled at her.' Because it wasn't Hayley Brown who tried to escape tonight. It was me. Tyler Lawless!'

****

Jazz and Charlie were in the kitchen drinking hot chocolate when the doorbell rang. Charlie stiffened. Jazz put her fingers to her lips to tell her to be quiet. She heard her mother shuffle to the door in her fluffy slippers. 'I wonder who that can be?' she was muttering.

Jazz held her breath. Something told her,(was it that psychic ability she was sure she had?) something told her it was the police. And they'd come for Charlie.

They both heard the voices at the door. Official voices, though the words were indistinct . Charlie realised who it was then. She began to panic. She stood up, ready to run. ' I'm not going back, I'm not going back.'

Two police women came in, and with them was Sister Phil. She reached out for Charlie and her voice was gentle.' You're not in any trouble, Charlie. I won't let anything happen to you. ' Her voice was gentle .

Jazz stepped in front of her. ' She's been threatened in that place. You can't take her back there. Can't she just stay here for the night?'

' I'm afraid not, Jazz,' Sister Phil said. ' But I promise you, we will look after her. She'll be in a room, on her own, well away from the other girls. You can come and see her on Saturday.'

' You said that before, but she was still threatened.' Jazz didn't budge from the spot. ' Why can't she just stay here for tonight.'

Charlie began to cry. One of the policewomen took her arm. ' Come on, honey,' she said gently. 'Someone will stay with you all night. I promise, you'll be fine.'

Jazz felt like crying too. She was worse than useless. She couldn't stop them.

Charlie threw herself into Jazz's arms, sobbing. ' Don't let them take me back there! Please Jazz.' Jazz grabbed Sister Phil. She tried to make her voice a whisper. ' She says she'll kill herself if she goes back.' She wanted them to know how serious she was.

Sister Phil's voice was reassuring, but nothing could reassure Jazz now. 'Someone will stay with her all night, and tomorrow. We know how to deal with these things.'

And Jazz could do nothing as she watched Sister Phil slide her arm round Charlie's shoulder, gently but firmly. Charlie almost had to be dragged out after that, and Jazz with her, for she never let go of Jazz's hand till they got to the front door.

' Who told you she was here? How did you know?'

Jazz dreaded the answer, already knew what it would be, yet it still stunned her. 'Your friend, Tyler Lawless, she called us. And don't be annoyed with her. She was worried about you, frightened you might get into trouble. She was worried about Charlie too. She did it for the best.'

CHAPTER 33

Jazz tried to call Tyler that night, but she didn't answer, or wouldn't answer her phone. Guilt, thought Jazz, or shame. And she should be ashamed. They should have helped Charlie. Not betray her.

And Jazz was not going to let this go.

She was waiting at the school gates for Tyler. Tyler spotted her as soon as she stepped from her bus. ' I know what you're going to say,' Tyler said at once, walking right past her, holding her hand out in a ' speak to the hand' gesture, not breaking her stride.

That really riled Jazz. She pulled her round to face her. ' I wish you had seen Charlie last night when they were dragging her out. She broke her heart. You did that, Tyler. You know what she said...she might kill herself if she goes back there. Don't you care about that?'

Tyler yanked her arm free. ' She was being a total drama queen. It was better for her to go back. And it was better for us. And I knew you were too much of a wimp to make that decision.'

' Wha...what did you call me?'

Tyler's mouth turned up in a sneer. What had happened to her to make her change so much? Jazz couldn't understand, but she was angry now. ' I said...what did you call me?'

Tyler brought her face close to Jazz's. ' Wimp! Wimp! Wimp!'

Jazz couldn't stop herself. She grabbed at Tyler's hair and pulled. Tyler grabbed at her wrists, then she lifted her foot and kicked Jazz on the shin.

A second later they were on the ground, punching, kicking, biting. And even in the heat of it, Jazz kept thinking. 'I'm fighting with my best friend. I'm fighting with Tyler.'

They were lifted to their feet. Jazz had scratches on her face, Tyler's hair was wild. Jazz had never seen her so angry. But then, she had never seen Tyler angry at all.

' You two! Rector's office! Now!'

****

So many thoughts tumbled through my head as I lay in my bed that night. So Hayley wasn't the poor unwanted loveless child I had thought her. Of course she wasn't. Charlie had lied. Charlie always lied. And I had believed her, and so had Jazz.

Jazz. My thoughts kept going back to her. If only there was some way to reach her, she would help.

And I wondered if she saw the difference between me and the new Tyler?

And what was Hayley doing to my life?

It had been a hopeless hope that Doctor Crow might believe me. She knew Hayley to be devious and evil. Bad to the bone, she said. She knew she would use any means to get out of here. And now, I would do the same.

So, how could I change things?

I would be very calm. Quiet, I wouldn't scream or shout, I wanted out of this room before Saturday. Saturday was my deadline. Hayley Brown was to die on Saturday. They wouldn't let me out unless I behaved.

I pictured them watching me through the spyhole in the door, checking my behaviour, checking that I wasn't self harming again.

I would show them. I would sit here, quiet as a mouse. Let them watch me. They would say, she wouldn't harm a fly, we can't keep her in there...and I would be free.

And I wondered if this was how all prisoners felt. The terror of hearing that door lock behind them, the walls closing in, the feeling of despair knowing there was no way out.

CHAPTER 34

Tyler and Jazz didn't talk all day. The others tried to get them together, especially Aisha, the peacemaker. ' It's not like Tyler, Jazz. Maybe she did think she was doing the right thing.'

And to Tyler she said. ' Jazz is a great friend, Tyler, you don't want to lose her.'

But even with all her efforts, after their visit to the Rector's office and a warning about fighting, they stayed well apart.

Until the afternoon that is, when they were both summoned once more the Rector's office.

' If this is me getting into more trouble because of you, Tyler, I'll really make you sorry.' Jazz warned as they marched to the office, side by side, but not together.

' Because of me!' Tyler snapped. ' I wasn't the one who was harbouring a fugitive!'

But the person who was waiting for them in the Rector's office was almost the last person Jazz expected to see.

Doctor Crow.

' What are you doing here!' It was Tyler who asked it, angrily. Too angrily. Jazz looked at her. Tyler's face was red with anger.

But she wanted to know too.' What *are* you doing here, Doctor Crow?'

The rector said. ' Sit down, girls. Doctor Crow has something to tell you. I believe you've met already.'

They sat down. Doctor Crow took a seat across from both girls. ' I'm sorry about coming to your school, but I thought it was better than going to your homes. I've been thinking and thinking about Hayley Brown since your visit. Something kept niggling at me. And I couldn't remember what it was. It only came to me this morning.' The doctor looked directly at Tyler. ' Your name is Tyler Lawless, isn't it?'

It was Jazz who answered. ' Yes, Tyler Lawless, and when you heard her name before, I saw your reaction.'

The doctor nodded. ' Yes. The name struck me, I couldn't think why. Until this morning when it suddenly came to me.' She looked again at Tyler. ' There was a time, just a short time, just before she died, when Hayley Brown claimed *she* was Tyler Lawless.'

****

It was morning before the door was opened again. I was already up, and determined to be on my best behaviour. I was all apologies. ' Good morning, Sister. I'm so sorry about last night. Don't know what came over me. I promise I'll behave today.'

Sister Angela smiled. ' Good morning, Hayley.'

How I hated being called that. But I didn't correct her. I smiled back. ' Could I have my breakfast with the other girls?'

She didn't say yes. ' I think you should have breakfast here, and then have a shower and I think the doctor wants to speak to you too.' Dismay must have shown on my face. ' How about lunch. I'll see what I can do about that?'

I could cope with that. ' Thank you, Sister.'

CHAPTER 35

Jazz still couldn't take it in. ' She said she was Tyler Lawless?'

' She was quite violent about it. Kept on and on that she wasn't Hayley Brown, she was Tyler Lawless.'

Jazz turned to Tyler. ' Do you hear that Tyler? Isn't that amazing!'

Tyler hardly glanced at her. ' Amazing.' But Tyler didn't look amazed.

' But Tyler Lawless is an unusual name, why did she chose that one?' Jazz kept her eyes on Tyler, watching for her response.

' It is unusual, I suppose that's why I remembered it,' Doctor Crow said. 'Although it had gone out of my head completely until you turned up, Tyler.'

Tyler still only glanced at the doctor. 'Some coincidence, eh?' she said dryly.

' Perhaps this Hayley Brown knew another Tyler Lawless, have you a relative of that name, Tyler?' The doctor asked.

' Must have,' Tyler said dismissively.

' Do you really think it's just a coincidence?' Jazz asked her.

Tyler turned on her. ' Of course it's a coincidence!' she snapped. ' What else could it be? You got another explanation?'

' Tyler, I don't understand you.' Jazz wasn't even angry. She was too puzzled to be angry. ' You don't seem surprised, and this is the kind of story you usually love.'

There was a moment's pause. ' How would you feel if it had been your name she used, think about that!'

The rector stepped in, saw things were getting out of hand. ' Enough you two!' He spoke to Doctor Crow. 'These girls are usually the best of friends, yet they were caught fighting like cats at the school gates this morning.' He turned to the girls. ' Now, come on, make up.'

Jazz looked at Tyler. Tyler leaned across and touched her hand. ' I'm so sorry, Jazz. All this has taken me by surprise. Give me time.'

At that moment, Jazz wanted to remind her what she'd done to Charlie-because it seemed to Jazz she'd forgotten all about it.

' There, Jazz, Tyler's apologised, ' the rector said. He was waiting for her apology.

She was mixed up, needed time to think, but she apologised anyway. ' Sorry, Tyler.'

Doctor Crow stood up. ' I simply wanted to let you know this. Especially when you showed such an interest in her. ' She spoke to Tyler. ' You like writing stories, don't you? Well, if you were writing a story about Hayley Brown, I think this adds what they call 'the shiver factor' don't you?'

The shiver factor. That's what Jazz thought as she walked back to class. Tyler didn't say a word to her, and she didn't speak to Tyler. A thought was growing in her mind, unbelievable, absurd, but it wouldn't go away.

A thought that would explain everything that was wrong with Tyler.

CHAPTER 34

By lunchtime I had spent the morning sitting in my room like an angel. Quiet and calm, apologising over and over for trying to get away and for all the bother I had caused. Trying to sound as reasonable and calm as I could. And by lunchtime it seemed to have worked. It was decided that I could leave the room, cross to the big house, eat with the other girls. I would be well guarded, but at least I could leave this room.

To hear that door being opened, to know I could walk through it, even only for a little while, was like a breath of heaven to me.

I was flanked by a nun and the burly warder as we walked across the lawns. How different it looked, in this time, in the past. It actually looked surprisingly more unkempt than it did in the future. It needed painted, the gardens needed tended to. Even the graveyard was overgrown. No Charlie to help look after it. They took me into the kitchen first. And there was Annie at the cooker, stirring something steaming in a pot. She was younger, slimmer, but as soon as she opened her mouth I knew she was till the same old Annie. She took one scornful look at me and said. ' 'Keep that one away from my hot soup. And anything sharp.'

And I couldn't help it, I smiled.

' Look! The wee so and so's laughing at me!'

' Oh Annie,' Sister Angelus scolded. And Annie turned back to her pot sullenly. Only the nuns and myself were there, apart from the warder who remained at my side.

' Bell hasn't run for lunch yet,' Sister said. ' We'll just wait here for the moment till the rest of the girls are seated.'

I smiled gratefully and she placed a hand on my shoulder. ' This is the way it could always be, Hayley.'

I so wanted to tell her I wasn't Hayley, but I said nothing, because to deny it would mean being put back in that locked room, and I couldn't risk that. At that moment, I felt I would never be Tyler again. I blinked back tears. What could I do? What could I possibly do? Despair was seeping into my very soul, and I didn't want it to. I sent a prayer through time. ' Jazz, find a way to help me, please. You're my only hope.'

A door opened behind me. ' Oh, look who we have here,' Sister Angelus said, sounding delighted.

I turned and one of the other Sisters came into the kitchen, carrying a baby. She was the cutest little thing I had ever seen, all dressed in a knitted pink suit. The baby was giggling, her chubby face bright with happiness. She was passed to another Sister, who held her high and when she dribbled onto the nun's face, she only laughed.

' And how's our darling this morning?' It was Annie who said it, cynical Annie, beaming a smile at this baby.

' We have to make the most of her, Annie. She'll be leaving us in a couple of days.'

The baby looked at me, and smiled. Even in the depths of my depression it was impossible not to smile back at the cherubic little face.

' Where is she going?' I asked.

' Going off to her new home,' Sister said.

' She is gorgeous,' With her perfect little rosebud mouth, and rosy cheeks, a big blue eyes, she was the kind of baby you just wanted to reach out and cuddle. And she knew it, her smile said she knew how loved she was.

' Isn't she just?' Sister Angelus said. 'We are going to miss her.'

' What's her name?' I asked.

' You know that, Hayley!' she scolded. But she wasn't angry. 'This is Charlotte,' she said, ' but we all call her Charlie.'

****

Jazz couldn't believe what she was thinking. It was impossible. She had too much imagination, that was it. She was making up one of Tyler's stories. Yet every time she thought it over, this was the only conclusion she could come to.

Something had happened to Tyler the last time they went to Bonaventure House. That much was definite.

Hadn't she seen the difference in her even that day? The way she danced down the drive, giggling for no apparent reason. And refusing to tell her what had happened with Hayley Brown.

And since then?

Every day something had changed about Tyler- the way she wore her hair, the make up, the vanity that was never a part of Tyler. The lies. Not like Tyler at all.

Even her mother had noticed the difference.

And the final straw, to have Charlie, sweet Charlie, dragged back like a criminal, back to a place she was terrified of being in, and to show no remorse for it. That was definitely not Tyler.

And then today?

That had been the final thing. Jazz had watched Tyler's reaction when Dr Crow had told her that Hayley Brown, all those years before Tyler had even been born, Hayley Brown had claimed to be Tyler Lawless. Not a blink of surprise. If anything, the only expression that appeared on her face, was annoyance.

This was a totally amazing story. Normally, she would have seen Tyler scribbling it down in a notebook as soon as they had left the office, not wanting to forget it. Her excitement would have lasted all day. She would not have been able to stop gabbling about it.

Yet, she had said nothing. Nothing. Almost as if it was no surprise to her. Almost as if she knew it already.

Almost as if she knew it already.

If Tyler had been writing this in a story, Jazz knew what she would say-that in some amazing way Hayley Brown had taken her over-become her-that day at Bonaventure House, and that this Tyler was really Hayley Brown.

And the real Tyler was trapped in the past, fifteen years in the past-in Hayley Brown's body.

If Tyler was writing this in a story.

But this was real life. Something like that could never happen.

Could it?

CHAPTER 35

' This is....Charlie?' I still couldn't believe what I was hearing, seeing. This bouncy, healthy, happy baby would grow up to be the pale, unhappy girl I had met only a couple of weeks ago. I wanted to hold her, hug her. I wanted to cry, knowing what the future held for her. Charlie.

' And we're going to lose her.'

' Lose her?' I asked.

' Oh we can't be sad about that, Hayley. She's being adopted . She's going to have such a lovely life.'

But Charlie wouldn't have a lovely life. I knew exactly the kind of life she would have.

Wait a minute, my mind was moving fast. Charlie had told us she had a lovely family and she had let them down.

But those were the words Sister had used to describe Hayley Brown's family life.

And what was it she had said about Hayley? What if Charlie had taken Hayley's life, the memory of a loving family who cared about her, and had given Hayley hers, the couple meant to adopt her, dying before they could sign the final papers, in and out of foster homes and children's homes. Her life spiralling out of control.

This baby, this little Charlotte, was the one with the horrible family, who didn't want her. Now she was to be adopted by a couple who loved her. I was trying to remember the rest of her story.

' When is she leaving?' I stammered over the words.

Sister didn't answer me. The lunch bell rang. I dutifully followed her into the lunch hall. Some girls were already in the hall, sitting at tables. They eyed me warily. I was the notorious Hayley Brown, or at least they thought I was. Mad, they said, and now I was claiming to be someone else, no wonder they thought I was mad. I imagined the sound died at once as they all looked at me. I sensed that no one wanted me to share their table.

Sister moved someone and sat me down. She patted my shoulder, bent and whispered. ' Don't let me down, Hayley.'

'I'm not Hayley!' I wanted to shout, but I said nothing. I ate my lunch silently. No one spoke to me, and I spoke to no one.

Lunch was almost over when there were cries of oos and aahs and I looked up and it was Charlie, much loved it seemed by all the girls, some of them jumped up, and hurried towards her. Charlie was in the arms of a young woman. A beaming young man stood behind them.

' Charlotte is leaving us tomorrow, girls.' Sister said.

There were cries of disappointment.

' Oh, I wish we could take her home today,' the young woman said.

' One more day,' said Sister. ' The papers will be signed and you can take her home. You've waited so long, you can surely wait one more day.'

One more day. What was it Charlie had said about the couple who were going to adopt Hayley?

She had told us that the day before they were due to take her home they had been killed in a freak accident, a runaway lorry had crashed into the gates of the school just as they were leaving, the lorry had hit their car, crushed it. They had both died.

The day before they were due to take her? Was this the day?

The woman handed little Charlie over reluctantly. ' We're just putting the finishing touches to her nursery,' she said to the girls. ' I'll send you a photo, I think she's going to love it.' She kissed Charlie then, and little Charlie's chubby fingers curled round her hair and wouldn't let go.

' Don't let go, Charlie,' I wanted to cry out. ' Don't ever let them go.'

But they were leaving. Charlie was finally handed to Sister Angelus. The couple were leaving and they didn't know that they had only minutes to live. They would drive out of here and their car would collide with that runaway lorry and Charlie's rosy future would be destroyed.

No!!!

I couldn't let that happen. I had to stop them leaving. A few minutes would make all the difference. A few minutes would save them. The truck would roar past, and hit the wall, and they would be safe, still here, and Charlie's future would be safe too.

I had to stop them leaving. But how?

CHAPTER 36

Jazz's phone rang that night and she was surprised to see it was Tyler's number. She'd wanted to call Tyler since she came home from school, but didn't know what to say. She answered at once

Tyler's voice was breathless and she sounded excited. ' Guess where I've been?' she said, and not waiting for an answer or expecting one she went on. ' I went to Doctor Crow's house. I couldn't stop thinking about what she said, Jazz. I mean it was an amazing story. Didn't you think so too? I had to see her again, talk to her about it.'

' We could have gone together,' Jazz said.

' Couldn't wait. Had to find out if she knew anything else.'

This, at least, was more like the old Tyler. And Jazz began to think that maybe she'd been wrong. ' And what did she say?'

' Doctor Crow can't understand it either. But she thinks there would be records at the school that might tell us more. She recorded everything when she was there.'

This was the response Jazz had expected from Tyler in the first place, curious, excited, and yet... it still bothered her.

' So,' Tyler went on, ' we'll go tomorrow, back to Bonaventure House. See what we can find out. We want to see Charlie anyway. I so have to apologise to her. Two birds with one stone.'

If Charlie wants to see us that is, Jazz thought.

' So, we'll go tomorrow? Usual time?'

Jazz agreed. She knew she had no choice. ' Yes, we'll go tomorrow.'

When she came off the phone she knew she should feel better. But there was still a knot in the middle of her stomach that told her something was wrong about all this. That Tyler had some kind of ulterior motive for going back to Bonaventure House. And she had a terrible feeling she knew what that something was. But it was impossible. But there was only one way to find out. Finally, she phoned Doctor Crow.

' Your friend was here,' the doctor said as soon as she answered.

' I know,' Jazz said.

' Was there something she forgot?'

Jazz took a deep breath. ' We were just wondering exactly when Hayley Brown died.'

There was a pause. Doctor Crow didn't want to answer that, but she did. ' Fifteen years ago,' she said. ' In fact, fifteen years ago tomorrow. November 27th. That's her anniversary.'

CHAPTER 37

Charlie was still in Sister Angela's arms. The woman still played with Charlie's face, running her fingers gently up and down her cheek. As if she couldn't bear to leave her be. They were all laughing, thinking this was their last day without Charlie. They didn't know it was their last day. Period.

I had to do something.

I stopped thinking about it. I reacted. I thought like Hayley Brown. I moved closer to Charlie, as discreetly as I could, as if I too wanted to brush my fingers across those chubby cheeks, and then, another step closer, and with one swoop, I had Charlie in my arms.

No one had expected it. Everyone was taken by surprise. Some of the girls screamed. The nuns reached out as if they would take her out of my arms. My burly bodyguard was held back as she sprang at me. They were all afraid I would hurt Charlie. There were angry yells. I held Charlie tight against me, and backed against the wall so no one could get behind me. They all turned to me. Surprise grew into horror.

' Hayley, put Charlie down.'

Charlie still giggled in my arms, looking up at me, all innocence. I shook my head.

One of the girls darted towards me. The young woman screamed. 'No! Please! She might hurt her.'

Of course, they thought I might hurt her. I was Hayley Brown , and why wouldn't they think that? I had pushed my own brother down a flight of stairs. Bad to the bone, I was relying on them believing Hayley Brown could hurt Charlie.

The woman began to step slowly forward. ' Please, Hayley. Give me Charlie. She's only a baby.'

I shook my head. Not yet, I thought. I had to wait.

' What are you doing, Hayley!' Sister Angela was angry, she had trusted me and I had let her down. ' What is the point of this!'

I could see disappointment in her eyes as well as anger. I'd be locked up again after this, locked up in that room I hated. The room I was due to die in tomorrow. I staggered further against the wall. Everyone gasped, afraid I might fall with the baby. I said nothing. I didn't know what to say. I was trembling all over. Everyone stood still, except the young woman. In a day she would be Charlie's mother. If only she knew that all I was doing was trying to help her. She took another step toward me. 'Please Hayley, she's my baby.'

And now Charlie reached out to her. Her chubby little fingers stretched out towards her. She wanted her mother. She began to struggle in my arms. But I held her tight. ' Get back!' I shouted.

The woman froze. Charlie began to cry.

' What is it you want, Hayley?' Sister Angela asked.

' I want out of here,' I said.

' I'll get you out. I'll help you.' The young woman said.

' So will I,' her husband stepped forward. ' I'm a lawyer. I can help you.'

' I want out today.'

' You're going the wrong way about it, Hayley. This is serious what you're doing here.'

None of the girls said a word. Too afraid for Charlie's safety to say or do anything. But I could see such hate in their eyes.

' Please Hayley,' the young woman was trying not to cry. Charlie's cries rang out in the crowded hall.

I don't know how long we all stood there. Saying nothing, doing nothing. More staff ran into the dining room, security men came in and were held back from coming towards me. Everyone had hate, nothing but hate for me in their eyes as they watched me. I would have stood there all day if I had to. I had to hold on. I had to be sure that couple were safe.

And then, in the distance I heard a roar, and a crash, a horrendous crash. Everyone jumped.

' What was that!' Sister Angela shouted. She ran to the door.

But I knew what it was- because with that roar there was a rush of wind. I felt dizzy, the room swayed around me. I knew what was happening. I had changed the past again.

That lorry had crashed, but the young couple who had been planning to adopt Charlie were still here. They hadn't left, they hadn't died and tomorrow they would come back and take Charlie home with them, and Charlie's life would be wonderful. And all of this because of me. No matter what happened now, I thought, if I had to stay here forever, if I had to die tomorrow, it would all have been worth it.

I held Charlie out to the woman. ' I only wanted to hold her,' I said.

She snatched her from me and as soon as Charlie was safe a crowd of the girls leapt on me and before they could be stopped they were punching me, kicking me, thumping me. It took several of the Sisters to pull them off.

And I was dragged away, back to that locked room.

' Look at her!' one of the girls said. ' She's smiling. She is evil.'

And yes, I was smiling, because I had changed Charlie's life.

CHAPTER 38

Tyler was nervous all the way to Bonaventure House next day. She was silent on the bus, didn't say a word, not like Tyler at all. Jazz watched her, tried to convince herself it was because she was nervous about what she might find out about Hayley Brown, and why she'd used her name all those years ago.

' I'll go and find everything out myself in the office. You go and get us a coffee,' Tyler said as they were stepping off the bus.

'No, I'll come with you,' Jazz said, determined not to leave her on her own. She wanted to see what she was going to do.

Tyler nodded, reluctantly. ' Let's go for a coffee first. I'm scared, Jazz. I have to know what this is all about, don't you?'

And that sounded more like Tyler. Was Jazz wrong about her? She had to be wrong, because it was too crazy to be the truth. She was so mixed up. If only she knew what was the truth.

' Yeah, let's do that.' Jazz said.

They sat in the coffee shop and talked and Tyler said all the things Jazz would have expected her to say. That she was scared, she didn't know how Hayley Brown could have used her name. She was afraid of what she was going to find out.

'Did you know she died fifteen years ago today?' Jazz had been trying to pick the right time to throw that one into the conversation.

Little splashes of red on her cheeks gave her away. She had known. But she shook her head. 'You're joking. Goodness, that is even more spooky, isn't it?' And Jazz was suspicious again. Finally, Tyler stood up. ' I'm going to the loo, when I come back, we'll go together to the records office, okay?'

Jazz nodded. Watched her as she walked the length of the cafe and turned at the door. She waved and smiled at Jazz. This was surely her old

Tyler back again? Worried, curious, afraid. Because what she was thinking was so unbelievable. Jazz played with her drink, wishing she knew what would be the right thing to do. She kept glancing at the door, waiting for Tyler to come back. Then, they'd go to the records office and they would find out the truth.

Jazz's phone rang. It was Tyler's mum. ' Are you at Bonaventure house, Jazz? Is Tyler with you?'

' Yes, she's just gone to the loo. Did you call her?'

'No. I wanted to call you first.' Mrs. Lawless sounded nervous. ' I've just had that Doctor Crow on the phone. She says Tyler was at her house.'

' Oh, I know, Mrs. Lawless. Tyler told me about it.'

She heard Mrs. Lawless take a deep breath. ' I'm really worried , Jazz. Did she tell you she stole something when she was there?'

' Stole something. Tyler would never steal anything.'

' I know, that's what I said.'

Jazz paused. ' What did she steal, Mrs. Lawless?'

' She stole one of Doctor Crow's knives.'

' Why would she do that, Jazz?' Tyler's mum had asked her.

'I don't know,' Jazz had said, and yet, she was so afraid that , in fact, she did know.

' This isn't like my Tyler, Jazz. It's not like her at all.'

No, this wasn't like Tyler, Jazz admitted it at last. No matter how crazy it sounded, this wasn't like Tyler, because, this wasn't Tyler.

It was as if a jigsaw was falling into place, but creating such a bizarre picture Jazz was sure she must have put it together wrong. Jazz looked over at the door of the cafe. There was no sign of Tyler returning. She was taking too long. And another piece fell into place. Tyler wasn't coming back.

Why had she stolen Doctor Crow's knife? Jazz stood up, began to walk to the door. There was a feeling deep inside her that something was going to happen. Yet, what could Tyler possibly do? What good was that knife to her today, in the present?

Tyler wasn't in the toilet. Jazz called out her name and her voice echoed around the walls. The cubicles were all empty. Just as she had known they would be.

Where had she gone? Yet, Jazz knew. It was raining hard now, steel spikes bouncing off the path, soaking into the ground. No one was about, everyone was sheltering from the downpour. Jazz ran to the window and stared at that little separate house, the one with the locked room. The room Hayley Brown had died in.

She knew that was where Tyler had gone. She was there in that house with Doctor Crow's knife in her pocket.

Hayley Brown had died in a locked room in that house, stabbed with Dr. Crow's knife. Suicide, everyone had said. But always with a question mark over that verdict. No one had ever known how she had got the knife. A doctor's career had been ruined because of it.

Who had told them all of that? Jazz couldn't remember, Sister Phil probably.

But Hayley Brown died a long time ago. Fifteen years ago. Fifteen years ago, today.

It was impossible what Jazz was thinking. That in some bizarre way, Tyler and Hayley Brown had swapped places, sometime last Saturday. And now Tyler was trapped in Hayley's body and in Hayley's time. She was trapped in that locked room, and now, Hayley, the real Hayley was heading her way, to fulfil the end of Hayley's story. No one had ever found out how the knife had got into the locked room.

Did Jazz know? Was that really what she was thinking? That the knife had come from the future. Now.

And it hadn't been suicide. It had been murder.

But it wasn't Hayley Brown who had died.

It had been Tyler Lawless.

CHAPTER 39

The sky grew dark. I could hear the rain battering against the window. How much time had passed since they had brought me back here. I had slept intermittently but all my dreams were nightmares. I was in real trouble now, after grabbing Charlie. As if anything worse than this could happen.

And today, unless I was wrong, was the day I was going to die.

I heard footsteps in the hallway. They stopped at my door. I felt as if someone was listening there. Ear pressed against the wood. Was it one of the Sisters, listening for me?

I got to my feet, and waited. The door opened.

And there she stood.

Or, there I stood.

I was looking at myself once again. At Tyler Lawless. My hair was different. It looked as if I was wearing lipstick. Me? I could say nothing. She saw me. I saw her. She in my time. Me in hers.

She was smiling. Had my smile ever held so much cruelty. ' Like being locked up?' she said, and it was my voice, not hers.

I glanced at the open door. ' I'm not locked up now.'

' We'll see.'

My mind was racing. Now was my chance to get my body back. If she could do it. So could I. I could make a run at her, grab her. I would force myself inside her, go through her, past her. Wasn't that all she'd done?

I couldn't let this chance go.

' Do you know how long I waited for you, Tyler?' she asked me.

' For me?'

' For you? For Tyler Lawless. They all wait for you. One the other side. They all wait because you're the one who can help them.'

' They wait for me?'

' All of them trying to get through to you. Jostling for position. We're the ones who weren't meant to die, and we know you can change that.'

She began to move round the room. Never taking her eyes from me.

' You weren't meant to die? Then I can save you...but not like this....'

' Oh, you mean you could save me, so I could live....?' She laughed a cruel laugh. Looked around the room. ' But live on here? Locked up? Trapped? There was no way I wanted that. So I figured out another way. I could get you to come here...' her voice, my voice became a piteous cry. " Help me, Tyler", so easy. You would come, and then... If I could become you and I could leave you here, take over your life...and you could die here, instead of me.' She smiled again. ' Clever, eh?'

She took something from her pocket. It gleamed in the dull light. It was a knife. 'Dr. Crow's knife.' She it said as if I had asked, holding the blade out to me. ' So easy to steal, when she thought I was sweet little Tyler Lawless. And thank you so much for finding out for me where she lived.'

232

And in that second I knew why she had come back. To fulfil her destiny. To die in a locked room, using Dr. Crow's knife, ruining the doctor's career and her life.

Only Hayley didn't intend that she should die. Not this time. This time I was the one who would die, in her body, in her time. Hayley was going to kill me.

And then she would carry on as me, living my life.

No! I was not giving up that easily. I threw myself at her, taking her by surprise. I knocked her off her feet. And this was when I knew I could have the upper hand. As Hayley Brown, I was bigger, older, used to fighting. She, as me, little Tyler Lawless, who didn't go in for fighting wouldn't stand a chance against me.

But then again, she had the knife. And if she was able to use it, plunge it into me, I would die. I would die as Hayley Brown. I reached for it, tried to grab it. She pulled away and the blade cut along my palm. We were both on the floor now. Then she punched me hard on the face. I punched back, Just as hard, and grabbed for the knife again. Finally, it flew away from her hand and rattled along the floor. She landed me another crack to my cheek and I rolled off her. She stretched across for the knife, but I could not let her get that knife. We both reached for it. Her foot came up, kicked me and sent me sprawling backwards. She almost touched it. Almost, but I grabbed her legs and yanked her away. She turned on me again. I saw my own face contorted with rage. The craziness of fighting with myself hit me. I took a second too long thinking of it and she punched me again on the nose this time, and I fell back, and felt blood spurt down my face.

Another piece of her destiny coming true. Hayley was found as if she had been involved in a terrible fight, well, here was why.

She was reaching for the knife again, and if she got it I was gone forever. I lunged at her-grabbed her hair, hauled it back. She turned to me and slapped me hard. My face stung, but I still held her. Then she butted me hard on the nose, I could taste blood in my throat, in my mouth. I felt dazed. For a split second my fingers loosened. She took that chance, stretched out for the knife. Another inch and she would have it. And I could do nothing to stop her. Nothing.

I knew then I had lost.

And just at that second. Jazz appeared at the door.

CHAPTER 40

Jazz stood at the door and looked around. The door was lying open. Why was the door of Room 4 lying open? Why had the door of the house been open? The room was empty. No one was here.

And yet....

Jazz had such a strange feeling. She could hear a sound in the distance. Was that outside? It was almost like faint voices? Crying out to her. She looked all around the room. It was empty, not a stick of furniture. Yet, she felt as if someone was here. Calling to her.

And then she saw the knife. Doctor Crow's knife, just lying there on the floor. But where was Tyler?

She called out her name. ' Tyler?'

And as if in answer, though the words were so faint they were surely only inside her head, she was sure she heard Tyler's voice.

' Help me, Jazz. Pick up the knife.'

She waited for another second.

Then she heard her voice again, pleading with her, breathless. ' Save me, Jazz. Please. Save me.'

She didn't understand what was happening. She probably never would. But she would not let Tyler down. Jazz bent and picked the knife up. It was heavy in her hand. It had been honed sharp, and...was that a line of blood on the blade? Jazz stood straight. That knife could not stay in this room. Wherever it went, it could not stay here. Not where Hayley Brown had died.

And Jazz turned and left the room.

****

' Nooooo!' Did Jazz hear that scream from Hayley? ' Noooooo!' A cry filled with desperation and anger. It burst through my eardrums and along with it there was a rush of wind, and the room swayed and I knew time was changing and I laughed.

' You're not going to die, Hayley. I've changed it. I've changed it. You are going to live.'

She grabbed my hair. Her voice was full of viciousness. ' Well, you're the one who is going to spend your life locked up in here!' She banged my head with such force I almost passed out. Then she punched me hard across the face. It seemed if I wasn't going to die in one way, she was going to kill me in another.

I stared into her face, into my face. ' Dream on, Hayley! You are going to live. And I am going back.' And with that I reached up and pulled her close. I wrapped my arms around her and I held her tight. She knew what I was going to do. I was going to do what she had done to me. And she struggled to stop me.

But now, I was stronger than she was. I was Hayley Brown in her body. She struggled with such force, we both rolled on the floor. But I held on. I felt myself go through her. And as I did I felt her agony and her pain and her fear. I heard her scream somewhere in the distance. Somewhere in the distance of time I heard her scream.

If only I could leave some hope for her. Some little part of me that loved life and people. But it seemed there was so much hate in Hayley there was no room for anything else. I pulled myself through her with every bit of strength I had and then, I was done. And I knew I had done it. I was free again.

I was me again.

I stumbled to my feet. Hayley still lay on the ground, battered, bruised and bloody. The way she had been found on the morning she died. But this time, she wasn't dead. And there was no knife.

She was crying. Banging on the floor, sobbing. Her plan hadn't worked. She was alive. There was no knife, and Doctor Crow's career was not in ruins.

' It's better this way, Hayley,' I said softly. Because suddenly I felt so sorry for her. ' You can make your life better. Only you can do that.'

Did she hear me? Did it matter? I didn't know. The room shimmered around me, and in a second I was standing in an empty room, and the door was lying wide open.

CHAPTER 41

Jazz was waiting for me when I came out of the house. Standing in the rain holding her umbrella. I felt like crying when I saw her. I wanted to run to her, to hug her. I was free, free to leave. Free to have my life again. She spun round when she heard me on the steps. ' There you are! I've been looking for you everywhere.' She glanced behind me towards the door of the house. ' I hope that's you finished with her.'

' Hayley Brown?' I nodded. ' I'm finished.'

' Look at the mess of you!' she began brushing me down. ' You look as if you've done ten rounds with Mike Tyson.' She looked into my eyes. ' What happened?'

I wished I could tell her everything. And perhaps one day I would find a way to do that. But that day wasn't now. Jazz would have no memory now of Charlie, or the girl who pretended to be me. I had changed all that when I had put things back the way they were meant to be.

Jazz smiled. ' I understand. You're special, Tyler. I don't know how, but I know you're special.'

' No, you're just as special, Jazz,' and I so wished that one day she would learn just how she had saved my life today.' Are you ready to go now?'

I was. Ready to go and never come back. But I longed to know if I had changed Hayley's life. I couldn't leave without finding that out. We went back into the office and I broached the subject with Sister Philomena.

' Hayley Brown? Well, we never really understood where all those bruises came from. It was as if she'd been in a terrible fight. But she never would tell us what happened. But you know something changed that night. It was as if the anger had been torn out of her. She became helpful, and thoughtful, and it wasn't too long after that she went back to stay with her parents. They thought we had worked some kind of miracle, but it wasn't us. It was Hayley Brown who had changed. '

'I'm so glad.' I said, and I was.

' I do have another theory,' Sister Phil said. ' That same day Hayley snatched a baby, right here in the dining room. Little Charlotte, she was about to be adopted and though I don't think there was any real badness intended,   Hayley could have been in terrible trouble about that, but the parents wouldn't have any charges brought against her. Because, and this is a strange thing, if they had left when they were meant to, they would have been involved in a horrendous accident, probably killed. In fact, Hayley snatching the baby actually saved their lives! She had changed their lives, she had changed Charlottes too. Little Charlotte has had such a happy life with that family. I think when Hayley learned that, it changed her whole attitude to life too.'

Maybe I *had* left a little bit of me inside Hayley after all, I thought. Or perhaps she had heard my whispered words. I hoped so.

Or maybe, I had just put things back the way they were meant to be.

That was all.

THE END

Tyler Lawless will be back in The Unexisted

Printed in Poland
by Amazon Fulfillment
Poland Sp. z o.o., Wrocław